CLASSIC
ADVENTURES

This book belongs to

Name ....

Date ....

Pinocchio

First published by J.M. Dent and Sons Ltd.
This facsimile edition
© Fabbri Publishing Ltd 1992
Printed and bound in Spain by Printer
Industria Gráfica, Barcelona

ISBN 1-85587-344-3

Pinocchio

By
Carlo Collodi

The Classic Adventures Series

I

ONE fine day a piece of wood was lying in the shop of an old carpenter of the name of Master Antonio. He was called by everybody Master Cherry, on account of the end of his nose, which was always as red and polished as a ripe cherry.

No sooner had Master Cherry set eyes on the piece of wood than his face beamed with delight ; and, rubbing his hands together with satisfaction, he said softly to himself : " This wood has come at the right moment ; it will just do to make the leg of a little table."

He immediately took a sharp axe, and just as he was going to give the first stroke he remained with his arm suspended in the air, for he heard a very small voice saying imploringly, " Do not strike me hard ! "

Picture to yourselves the astonishment of good old Master Cherry ! He turned his terrified eyes all round the room to try and discover where the little voice could possibly have come from, but he saw nobody ! He looked under the bench—nobody ; he looked into a cupboard that was always shut—nobody ; he looked into a basket of shavings and sawdust—nobody ; he even opened the door of the shop and gave a glance into the street—and still nobody. Who, then, could it be ?

" I see how it is," he said, laughing and scratching his wig ; " evidently that little voice was all my imagination. Let us set to work again." And taking up the axe he struck a tremendous blow on the piece of wood.

" Oh ! oh ! you have hurt me ! " cried the same little voice dolefully.

This time Master Cherry was petrified. As soon as he had recovered the use of his speech, he began to say, stuttering and trembling with fear : " But where on earth can that little voice have come from that said Oh ! oh ! ? . . . Is it possible that this piece of wood can have learnt to cry and to lament like a child ? I cannot believe it. If any one is hidden inside, so much the worse for him. I will settle him at once."

So saying, he seized the poor piece of wood and commenced beating it without mercy. Then he stopped to listen if he could hear any little voice lamenting. He waited two minutes—nothing ; five minutes—nothing ; ten minutes—still nothing !

" I see how it is," he then said, forcing himself to laugh and pushing up his wig ; " evidently the little voice that said Oh! oh! was all my imagination! Let us set to work again."

But as all the same he was in a great fright, he tried to sing to give himself a little courage. Putting the axe aside he took his plane, to plane and polish the bit of wood; but whilst he was running it up and down he heard the same little voice say, laughing, "Have done! you are tickling me all over!"

This time poor Master Cherry fell down as if he had been struck by lightning. When he at last opened his eyes he found himself seated on the floor.

At that moment some one knocked at the door.

"Come in," said the carpenter. A lively little old man immediately walked into the shop. His name was Geppetto, but when the boys of the neighbourhood wished to put him in a passion they called him by the nickname of Pudding-head because his yellow wig greatly resembled a pudding made of Indian corn.

Geppetto was very fiery. Woe to him who called him Pudding-head. He became furious, and there was no holding him.

"Good day, Master Antonio," said Geppetto; "what are you doing there on the floor?"

"I am teaching the alphabet to the ants."

"Much good may that do you."

"What has brought you to me, neighbour Geppetto?"

"My legs. I am come to ask a favour of you."

"Here I am, ready to serve you," replied the carpenter, getting on to his knees.

"This morning an idea came into my head. I thought I would make a beautiful wooden puppet; a wonderful puppet that should know how to dance, to fence, and to leap like an acrobat. With this puppet I would travel about the world to earn a piece of bread and a glass of wine. What do you think of it ?"

" Bravo, Pudding-head !" exclaimed the same little voice, and it was impossible to say where it came from.

Hearing himself called Pudding-head Geppetto became as red as a turkey-cock from rage, and turning to the carpenter he said in a fury : " Why do you insult me ?"

" Who insults you ?"

" You called me Pudding-head ! . . ."

" It was not I."

" Would you have it, then, that it was I ? It was you, I say !"

" No !"

" Yes !"

" No !"

" Yes !"

And becoming more and more angry, from words they came to blows, and flying at each other they bit, and fought, and scratched manfully. When the fight was over Master Antonio was in possession of Geppetto's yellow wig, and Geppetto discovered that the grey wig belonging to the carpenter had remained between his teeth.

" Give me back my wig," screamed Master Antonio.

" And you, return me mine, and let us make friends."

The two old men having each recovered his own wig shook hands, and swore that they would remain friends to the end of their lives.

" Well, then, neighbour Geppetto," said the carpenter, to prove that peace was made, " what is the favour that you wish of me ?"

" I want a little wood to make my puppet ; will you give me some ?"

Master Antonio was delighted, and he immediately

went to the bench and fetched the piece of wood that had caused him so much fear. But just as he was going to give it to his friend the piece of wood gave a shake, and wriggling violently out of his hands struck with all its force against the dried-up shins of poor Geppetto.

" Ah ! is that the courteous way in which you make your presents, Máster Antonio ? You have almost lamed me ! . . ."

" I swear to you that it was not I ! . . ."

" Then you would have it that it was I ? . . ."

" The wood is entirely to blame ! . . ."

" I know that it was the wood ; but it was you that hit my legs with it ! . . ."

" I did not hit you with it ! . . ."

" Liar ! "

" Geppetto, don't insult me or I will call you Pudding-head ! "

" Ass ! "

" Pudding-head ! "

" Donkey ! "

" Pudding-head ! "

" Baboon ! "

" Pudding-head ! "

On hearing himself called Pudding-head for the third time Geppetto, blind with rage, fell upon the carpenter and they fought desperately. Their accounts being thus squared they shook hands, and swore to remain good friends for the rest of their lives.

Geppetto carried off his fine piece of wood and, thanking Master Antonio, returned limping to his house.

II

As soon as he reached home Geppetto took his tools and set to work to cut out and model his puppet.

" What name shall I give him? " he said to himself; " I think I will call him Pinocchio. It is a name that will bring him luck. I once knew a whole family so called. There was Pinocchio the father, Pinocchia the mother, and Pinocchi the children, and all of them did well. The richest of them was a beggar."

Having found a name for his puppet he began to work in good earnest, and he first made his hair, then his forehead, and then his eyes. The eyes being finished, imagine his astonishment when he perceived that they moved and looked fixedly at him. Geppetto seeing himself stared at by those two wooden eyes took it almost in bad part, and said in an angry voice: " Wicked wooden eyes, why do you look at me? "

No one answered.

He then proceeded to carve the nose; but no sooner had he made it than it began to grow. And it grew, and grew, and grew, until in a few minutes it had become an immense nose that seemed as if it would never end. Poor Geppetto tired himself out with cutting it off; but the more he cut and shortened it, the longer did that impertinent nose become! The mouth was not even completed when it began to laugh and deride him.

"Stop laughing!" said Geppetto, provoked; but he might as well have spoken to the wall. "Stop laughing, I say!" he roared in a threatening tone. The mouth then ceased laughing, but put out its tongue as far as it would go. Geppetto, not to spoil his handiwork, pretended not to see, and continued his labours. After the mouth he fashioned the chin, then the throat, then the shoulders, the stomach, the arms and the hands. The hands were scarcely finished when Geppetto felt his wig snatched from his head. He turned round, and what did he see? He saw his yellow wig in the puppet's hand.

"Pinocchio! . . . Give me back my wig instantly!"

But Pinocchio, instead of returning it, put it on his own head, and was in consequence nearly smothered. Geppetto at this insolent and derisive behaviour felt sadder and more melancholy than he had ever been in his life before; and turning to Pinocchio he said to him: "You young rascal! You are not yet completed, and you are already beginning to show want of respect to your father! That is bad, my boy, very bad!" And he dried a tear.

The legs and the feet remained to be done. When Geppetto had finished the feet he received a kick on the point of his nose. "I deserve it!" he said to himself; "I should have thought of it sooner! Now it is too late!"

He then took the puppet under the arms and placed him on the floor to teach him to walk. When his legs became flexible Pinocchio began to walk by himself and to run about the room; until, having gone out of the house door, he jumped into the street and escaped. Poor Geppetto rushed after him but was not able to overtake him, for that rascal Pinocchio leapt in front of him like a hare, and knocking his wooden feet together against the pavement made as much clatter as twenty pairs of peasants' clogs.

" Stop him ! stop him ! " shouted Geppetto ; but the people in the street, seeing a wooden puppet running like a racehorse, stood still in astonishment to look at it, and laughed. At last a carabineer, hearing the uproar, imagined that a colt had escaped from his master. Planting himself courageously with his legs apart in the middle of the road, he waited with the determined purpose of stopping him, and thus preventing the chance of worse disasters.

When Pinocchio saw the carabineer barricading the whole street, he endeavoured to take him by surprise and to pass between his legs. But the carabineer without disturbing himself in the least caught him cleverly by the nose —it was an immense nose—and consigned him to Geppetto. Geppetto intended to pull his ears at once ; but imagine his feelings when he could not find them ! And do you know the reason ? It was that, in his hurry to model him, he had forgotten to make them.

Pinocchio threw himself on the ground and would not take another step. A crowd of idlers and inquisitive people began to assemble and to make a ring round them.

It ended in so much being said and done that the carabineer at last set Pinocchio at liberty and conducted Geppetto to prison.

Pinocchio, finding himself free from the clutches of the carabineer, ran off as fast as his legs could carry him.

Having arrived at the house he threw himself seated on the ground and gave a great sigh of satisfaction.

" Cri-cri-cri ! "

" Who calls me ? " said Pinocchio in a fright.

" It is I ! I am the Talking-cricket, and I have lived in this room a hundred years and more."

" Now, however, this room is mine," said the puppet, " and if you would do me a pleasure go away at once."

" I will not go," answered the Cricket, " until I have told you a great truth."

" Tell it me, then, and be quick about it."

" Woe to those boys who rebel against their parents, and run away from home. They will never come to any good in the world, and sooner or later they will repent bitterly."

" Sing away, Cricket, as you please, and as long as you please. For me, I have made up my mind to run away to-morrow at daybreak, because if I remain I shall not escape the fate of all other boys ; I shall be sent to school and shall be made to study ; but it is much more amusing to run after butterflies, or to climb trees and to take birds' nests."

" Poor little goose ! But do you not know that in that way you will grow up a perfect donkey, and that every one will make game of you ? "

" Hold your tongue, you wicked ill-omened croaker ! " shouted Pinocchio.

But the Cricket, who was patient and philosophical, instead of becoming angry at this impertinence, continued in the same tone :

" But if you do not wish to go to school why not at least learn a trade, if only to enable you to earn honestly a piece of bread ! "

" Do you want me to tell you ? " replied Pinocchio, who was beginning to lose patience. " Amongst all the trades in the world there is only one that really takes my fancy."

" And that trade—what is it ? "

" It is to eat, drink, sleep, and amuse myself, and to lead a vagabond life from morning to night."

" As a rule," said the Talking-cricket with the same composure, " all those who follow that trade end almost always either in a hospital or in prison."

" Take care, you wicked ill-omened croaker ! . . . Woe to you if I fly into a passion ! . . ."

" Poor Pinocchio !   I really pity you ! . . ."

" Why do you pity me ? "

" Because you are a puppet and, what is worse, because you have a wooden head."

At these last words Pinocchio jumped up in a rage, and snatching a wooden hammer from the bench he threw it at the Talking-cricket. Perhaps he never meant to hit him ; but unfortunately it struck him exactly on the head, so that the poor Cricket had scarcely breath to cry cri-cri-cri, and then he remained dried up and flattened against the wall.

Night was coming on, and Pinocchio, remembering that he had eaten nothing all day, began to feel hungry— a hunger that was really quite insupportable.

He then began to run about the room, searching in the drawers and in every imaginable place, in hopes of finding a bit of bread. If it was only a bit of dry bread, a crust, a bone left by a dog, a little mouldy pudding of Indian corn, a fish bone, a cherry stone—in fact anything that he could gnaw. But he could find nothing, nothing at all, absolutely nothing.

And in the meanwhile his hunger grew and grew ; and poor Pinocchio had no other relief than yawning, and his yawns were so tremendous that sometimes his mouth almost reached his ears. And after he had yawned he spluttered, and felt as if he was going to faint.

Recovering, however, from his stupefaction, he began to cry and scream, and to stamp his feet on the floor in desperation, and amidst his sobs he said : " Ah ! indeed the Talking-cricket was right. If I had not run away from home, and if my papa was here, I should not now be dying of hunger ! Oh ! what a dreadful illness hunger is ! . . ."

And as his stomach cried out more than ever and he did not know how to quiet it, he thought he would leave the house and make an excursion in the neighbourhood in hopes of finding some charitable person who would give him a piece of bread.

III

IT was a wild and stormy winter's night. The thunder was tremendous and the lightning so vivid that the sky seemed on fire. Pinocchio had a great fear of thunder, but hunger was stronger than fear. He therefore closed the house door and made a rush for the village ; but he found it all dark and deserted. The shops were closed, the windows shut, and there was not so much as a dog in the street. It seemed the land of the dead.

He returned home like a wet chicken quite exhausted with fatigue and hunger ; and having no longer strength to stand, he sat down and rested his damp and muddy feet on a brazier full of burning embers. And then he fell asleep ; and whilst he slept his feet, which were wooden, took fire, and little by little they burnt away and became cinders.

Pinocchio continued to sleep and to snore as if his feet belonged to some one else. At last about daybreak he awoke because some one was knocking at the door.

" Who is there ? " he asked, yawning and rubbing his eyes.

" It is I ! " answered a voice. And the voice was Geppetto's voice.

Poor Pinocchio had not as yet discovered that his feet were burnt off. The moment, therefore, that he slipped off his stool to run and open the door he fell his whole length on the floor.

" Open the door ! " shouted Geppetto from the street.

" Dear papa, I cannot," answered the puppet, crying and rolling about on the ground.

" Why cannot you ? "

" Because my feet have been eaten."

" And who has eaten your feet ? "

" The cat," said Pinocchio, seeing the cat, who was amusing herself by making some shavings dance with her forepaws. " I cannot stand up, believe me. Oh, poor me ! poor me ! I shall have to walk on my knees for the rest of my life ! . . ."

Geppetto, believing that all this lamentation was only another of the puppet's tricks, thought of a means of putting an end to it, and climbing up the wall he got in at the window. He was very angry ; but when he saw his Pinocchio lying on the ground and really without feet he was quite overcome. He took him in his arms and began to kiss and caress him and to say a thousand endearing things to him, and as the big tears ran down his cheeks, he said, sobbing :

" My little Pinocchio ! how did you manage to burn your feet ? "

" I don't know, papa, but believe me it has been a night that I shall remember as long as I live. It thundered and lightened, and I was very hungry, and then the Talking-cricket said to me : ' It serves you right ; you have been wicked and you deserve it,' and I said to him : ' Take care, Cricket ! ' . . . and he said : ' You are a puppet and you have a wooden head,' and I threw the handle of a hammer at him, and he died, and because I was very hungry I put my feet on the brazier to dry them, and then you returned, and I found they were burnt off, and I am always hungry, but I have no longer any feet !   Ih ! Ih ! Ih ! Ih ! . . ." And poor Pinocchio began to cry so loudly that he was heard miles off.

Geppetto, who from all this jumbled account had only understood one thing, which was that the puppet was dying of hunger, drew from his pocket three pears, and giving them to him said : " These three pears were intended for my breakfast ; but I will give them to you willingly."

" If you wish me to eat them, be kind enough to peel them for me."

" Peel them ? " said Geppetto, astonished. " I should never have thought, my boy, that you were so dainty and fastidious. That is bad ! In this world we should accustom ourselves from childhood to like and to eat everything, for there is no saying to what we may be brought."

" You are no doubt right, but I will never eat fruit that has not been peeled.   I cannot bear rind."

So that good Geppetto fetched a knife, and arming himself with patience peeled the three pears, and put the rind on a corner of the table.   Having eaten the first pear in two mouthfuls, Pinocchio was about to throw away the core ; but Geppetto caught hold of his arm and said to him : " Do not throw it away ; in this world everything may be of use."

" But core I am determined I will not eat."

"Who knows! there are so many chances! . . ." said Geppetto without losing his temper.

And so the three cores, instead of being thrown out of the window, were placed on the corner of the table together with the three rinds.

Having devoured the three pears, Pinocchio yawned, and then said in a fretful tone: "I am as hungry as ever!"

"But, my boy, I have nothing more to give you but the rind and the cores."

"One must have patience!" said Pinocchio; "if there is nothing else I will eat a rind." And he began to chew it. At first he made a wry face; but then one after another he quickly disposed of the rinds: and after the rinds even the cores, and then he said joyfully: "Ah! now I feel comfortable."

"You see now," observed Geppetto, "that I was right when I said to you that it did not do to accustom ourselves to be too particular or too dainty in our tastes. We can never know, my dear boy, what may happen to us. There are so many chances! . . ."

No sooner had the puppet appeased his hunger than he began to cry and to grumble because he wanted a pair of new feet. But Geppetto, to punish him for his naughtiness, allowed him to cry and to despair for half the day. He then said to him: "Why should I make you new feet? To enable you, perhaps, to escape again from home?"

"I promise you," said the puppet, sobbing, "that for the future I will be good."

"All boys," replied Geppetto, "when they are bent upon obtaining something, say the same thing."

"I promise you that I will go to school, and that I will study and earn a good character."

" All boys, when they are bent on obtaining something, repeat the same story."

" But I am not like other boys !   I am better than all of them and I always speak the truth.   I promise you, papa, that I will learn a trade, and that I will be the consolation and the staff of your old age."

Geppetto, although he put on a severe face, had his eyes full of tears and his heart big with sorrow at seeing his poor Pinocchio in such a pitiable state.   He did not say another word, but taking his tools and two small pieces of well-seasoned wood he set to work with great diligence.   In less than an hour the feet were finished :   two little feet—swift, well-knit, and nervous.   They might have been modelled by an artist of genius.   Geppetto then said to the puppet :
" Shut your eyes and go to sleep ! "

And Pinocchio shut his eyes and pretended to be asleep, whilst Geppetto, with a little glue which he had melted in an egg-shell, fastened his feet in their place, and it was so well done that not even a trace could be seen of where they were joined.

No sooner had the puppet discovered that he had feet than he jumped down from the table on which he was lying, and began to spring and to cut a thousand capers about the room, as if he had gone mad with the greatness of his delight.

" To reward you for what you have done for me," said Pinocchio to his father, " I will go to school at once."

" Good boy."

" But to go to school I shall want some clothes."

Geppetto, who was poor, and who had not so much as a farthing in his pocket, then made him a little dress of flowered paper, a pair of shoes from the bark of a tree, and a cap of the crumb of bread.

Pinocchio ran immediately to look at himself in a crock of water, and he was so pleased with his appearance that he said, strutting about like a peacock :

" I look quite like a gentleman ! "

" Yes indeed," answered Geppetto, " for bear in mind that it is not fine clothes that make the gentleman, but rather clean clothes."

" By the bye," added the puppet, " to go to school I shall want a Spelling-book."

" You are right : but what shall we do to get one ? "

" It is quite easy. We have only to go to the book-seller's and buy it."

" And the money ? "

" I have none."

" No more have I," added the good old man very sadly. And Pinocchio, although he was a very merry boy, became sad also ; because poverty, when it is real poverty, is understood by everybody—even by boys.

" Well, patience ! " exclaimed Geppetto, all at once rising to his feet ; and putting on his old fustian coat, all patched and darned, he ran out of the house.

He returned shortly, holding in his hand a Spelling-book for Pinocchio, but the old coat was gone. The poor man was in his shirt sleeves, and out of doors it was snowing.

" And the coat, papa ? "

" I have sold it."

" Why did you sell it ? "

" Because I found it too hot."

Pinocchio understood this answer in an instant, and unable to restrain the impulse of his good heart he sprang up, and throwing his arms round Geppetto's neck he began kissing him again and again.

IV

Pinocchio set out for school with his fine Spelling-book under his arm, and talking to himself he said : " To-day at school I will learn to read at once ; then to-morrow I will begin to write, and the day after to-morrow to cipher. Then with my acquirements I will earn a great deal of money, and with the first money I have in my pocket I will immediately buy for my papa a beautiful new cloth coat. To buy me books and have me taught he has remained in his shirt sleeves. . . . And in this cold ! It is only fathers who are capable of such sacrifices ! . . ."

Whilst he was saying this he thought that he heard music in the distance. He stopped and listened. The sounds came from the end of a cross street that led to a little village on the seashore.

" What can that music be ? What a pity that I have to go to school, or else . . ." And he remained irresolute. It was, however, necessary to come to a decision. Should he go to school ? or should he go after the music ?

" To-day I will go and hear the music, and to-morrow I will go to school," finally decided the young scapegrace, shrugging his shoulders. The more he ran the nearer came the sounds of the fifes and the beating of the big drum : fi-fi-fi, zum, zum, zum, zum.

At last he found himself in the middle of a square quite

24

full of people, who were all crowding round a building
made of wood and canvas, with a placard which read :

" GREAT PUPPET THEATRE."

" How much does it cost to go in ? " asked Pinocchio.

" Twopence."

Pinocchio, who was in a fever of curiosity, lost all
control of himself, and without any shame he said to the
little boy to whom he was talking :

" Would you lend me twopence until to-morrow ? "

" I would willingly," said the other, " but it so happens
that to-day I cannot."

" I will sell you my jacket for twopence," the puppet
then said to him.

" What do you think that I could do with a jacket of
flowered paper ?   If there was rain and it got wet, it would
be impossible to get it off my back."

" Will you buy my shoes ? "

" They would only be of use to light the fire."

" How much will you give me for my cap ? "

" That would be a wonderful acquisition indeed !
A cap of bread crumb !   There would be a risk of the mice
coming to eat it whilst it was on my head."

Pinocchio was on thorns.   He was on the point of making
another offer, but he had not the courage.   He hesitated,
felt irresolute and remorseful.   At last he said :

" Will you give me twopence for this new Spelling-
book ? "

" I am a boy and I don't buy from boys," replied his
little interlocutor, who had much more sense than he had.

" I will buy the Spelling-book for twopence," called out
a hawker of old clothes, who had been listening to the
conversation. And the book was sold there and then.

And to think that poor Geppetto had remained at home trembling with cold in his shirt sleeves, that he might buy his son a Spelling-book !

When Pinocchio came into the little puppet theatre Harlequin and Punchinello were as usual quarrelling with each other.

The audience laughed till they were ill.

All at once Harlequin stopped short, and turning to the public he pointed with his hand to some one far down in the pit, and exclaimed in a dramatic tone : " Do I dream, or am I awake ? But surely that is Pinocchio ! . . ."

" It is indeed Puncchio ! " cried Punchinello.

" It is indeed himself ! " screamed Miss Rose, peeping from behind the scenes.

" It is Pinocchio ! it is Pinocchio ! " shouted all the puppets in chorus, leaping from all sides on to the stage. " It is Pinocchio ! It is our brother Pinocchio ! Long live Pinocchio ! . . ."

" Pinocchio, come up here to me," cried Harlequin, " and throw yourself into the arms of your wooden brothers ! "

Pinocchio made a leap from the end of the pit into the reserved seats ; another leap landed him on the head of the leader of the orchestra, and he then sprang upon the stage. The embraces, the hugs, and the warm brotherly affection that Pinocchio received from the puppet dramatic company beat description. The public in the pit, finding that the play was stopped, became impatient, and began to shout : " Go on with the play ! " It was all breath thrown away. At that moment out came the showman. He was very big, and so ugly that the sight of him was enough to frighten any one. His beard was as black as ink, and so long that it reached from his chin to the ground.

I need only say that he trod upon it when he walked. His mouth was as big as an oven, and his eyes were like two lanterns of red glass with lights burning inside them. He carried a large whip made of snakes and foxes' tails twisted together, which he cracked constantly.

At his unexpected appearance there was a profound silence : no one dared to breathe.

" Why have you come to raise a disturbance in my theatre ? " asked the showman of Pinocchio.

" Believe me, honoured sir, that it was not my fault ! . . ."

" That is enough ! To-night we will settle our accounts."

As soon as the play was over the showman went into the kitchen where a sheep was turning slowly on the spit in front of the fire. He called Harlequin and Punchinello, and said to them : " Bring that puppet here : you will find him hanging on a nail. He is made of very dry wood. He would make a beautiful blaze for the roast."

The showman Fire-eater—for that was his name— had, however, not a bad heart. When he saw poor Pinocchio brought before him, struggling and screaming " I will not die, I will not die ! " he was quite moved and felt very sorry for him. He sneezed violently.

" Good news, brother," said Harlequin. " The show-man has sneezed, and that is a sign that he pities you, and consequently you are saved."

After he had sneezed, the showman shouted to Pinocchio: " Your lamentations have given me a pain in my stomach . . . Etci ! etci ! " and he sneezed again twice.

" Bless you ! " said Pinocchio.

" Thank you ! And your papa and your mamma, are they still alive ? " asked Fire-eater.

" Papa, yes ; my mamma I have never known."

" Who can say what a sorrow it would be for your poor old father if I was to have you thrown amongst those burning coals ! Poor old man ! I compassionate him ! . . . Etci ! etci ! etci ! " and he sneezed again three times.

" Bless you ! " said Pinocchio.

" Thank you ! All the same, I have no more wood with which to finish roasting my mutton. Instead of you I will burn under the spit one of the puppets belonging to my company. Ho there, gendarmes ! Take Harlequin, bind him securely, and then throw him on the fire to burn."

Only imagine that poor Harlequin ! His terror was so great that his legs bent under him, and he fell with his face on the ground.

At this Pinocchio, weeping bitterly, threw himself at the showman's feet, saying in a supplicating voice : " Have pity, Sir Fire - eater ! I implore you to pardon poor Harlequin."

" For him there can be no pardon. As I have spared you he must be put on the fire, for I am determined that my mutton shall be well roasted."

" In that case," cried Pinocchio proudly, " I know my duty. Come on, gendarmes ! Bind me and throw me amongst the flames. No, it is not just that poor Harlequin, my true friend, should die for me ! . . ."

These words, pronounced in a loud heroic voice, made all the puppets who were present cry.

Fire-eater at first remained as hard and unmoved as ice, but little by little he began to melt and to sneeze. And having sneezed four or five times, he opened his arms affectionately, and said to Pinocchio : " You are a good, brave boy ! Come here and give me a kiss."

Pinocchio ran at once, and deposited a hearty kiss on the point of his nose.

V

THE following day Fire-eater called Pinocchio on one side and asked him : " What is your father's name ? "

" Geppetto."

" And what trade does he follow ? "

" He is a beggar."

" Does he gain much ? "

" Gain much ? Why, he has never a penny in his pocket. Only think, to buy a Spelling-book for me to go to school he was obliged to sell his only coat."

" Poor devil ! I feel almost sorry for him ! Here are five gold pieces. Go at once and take them to him with my compliments."

You can easily understand that Pinocchio thanked the showman a thousand times. He embraced all the puppets of the company one by one, even to the gendarmes, and beside himself with delight set out to return home. But he had not gone far when he met on the road a Fox lame of one foot, and a Cat blind of both eyes, who were going along helping each other like good companions in misfortune. The Fox walked leaning on the Cat, and the Cat was guided by the Fox.

" Good day, Pinocchio," said the Fox, accosting him politely.

" How do you come to know my name ? " asked the puppet.

" I know your father well."

" Where did you see him ? "

" I saw him yesterday at the door of his house."

" And what was he doing ? "

" He was in his shirt sleeves and shivering with cold."

" Poor papa !   But that is over ; for the future he shall shiver no more ! . . ."

" Why ? "

" Because I am become a gentleman."

" A gentleman—you ! " said the Fox, and he began to laugh rudely and scornfully. The Cat also began to laugh, but to conceal it she combed her whiskers with her forepaws.

" There is little to laugh at," cried Pinocchio angrily. " If you know anything about it, you can see that these are five gold pieces." And he pulled out the money that Fire-eater had given him.

At the sympathetic ring of the money the Fox stretched out the paw that had seemed crippled, and the Cat opened wide two eyes that looked like two green lanterns. It is true that she shut them again, and so quickly that Pinocchio observed nothing.

" And now," asked the Fox, " what are you going to do with all that money ? "

" First of all," answered the puppet, " I intend to buy a new coat for my papa, and then I will buy a Spelling-book for myself ; for I wish to go to school to study in earnest."

" Look at me ! " said the Fox. " Through my foolish passion for study I have lost a leg."

" Look at me ! " said the Cat. " Through my foolish passion for study I have lost the sight of both my eyes."

At that moment a white Blackbird, that was perched on the hedge by the road, began his usual song, and said : " Pinocchio, don't listen to the advice of bad companions : if you do you will repent it ! . . ."

" Would you like to make out of your five miserable sovereigns, a hundred, a thousand, two thousand ? " said the Fox.

" I should think so ! but in what way ? "

" Go with us, to the land of the Owls."

Pinocchio reflected a moment, and then he said resolutely:

" No, I will not go.   I will return home to my papa who is waiting for me.   I have indeed been a bad son, and the Talking-cricket was right when he said : ' Disobedient boys never come to any good in the world.'   I have found it to my cost, for many misfortunes have happened to me. Even yesterday in Fire-eater's house I ran the risk. . . . Oh ! it makes me shudder only to think of it ! "

" Well, then," said the Fox, " you are quite decided to go home ?   Go, and so much the worse for you."

" So much the worse for you ! " repeated the Cat.

" Between to-day and to-morrow your five sovereigns would have become two thousand."

" Two thousand ! " repeated the Cat.

" But how is it possible ? " asked Pinocchio.

" I will explain it to you at once," said the Fox.   " You must know that in the land of the Owls there is a field called the Field of miracles.   In this field you must dig a little hole, and you put into it, we will say, one gold sovereign. You then cover up the hole with a little earth : you must water it with two pails of water from the fountain, then sprinkle it with two pinches of salt, and when night comes you can go quietly to bed. During the night, the gold piece will grow and flower, and in the morning when you get up and return to the field, you find a beautiful tree laden with as many gold sovereigns as a fine ear of corn has grains in the month of June."

" Oh ! how delightful ! " cried Pinocchio, dancing for joy. " As soon as ever I have obtained those sovereigns, I will keep two thousand for myself, and five hundred I will make a present of to you two."

" A present to us ? " cried the Fox with indignation and appearing much offended. " What are you dreaming of ? "

" What are you dreaming of ? " repeated the Cat.

" We do not work," said the Fox, " for dirty interest : we work solely to enrich others."

" Others ! " repeated the Cat.

" What good people ! " thought Pinocchio to himself : and forgetting there and then his papa, the new coat, the Spelling-book, and all his good resolutions, he said to the Fox and the Cat :

" Let us be off at once. I will go with you."

They walked and walked, until at last, towards evening, they arrived dead tired at the inn of The Red Craw-fish.

" Let us stop here a little," said the Fox, " for food and rest. We will start again at midnight, so as to arrive at the Field of miracles by dawn to-morrow morning."

When they had supped, the Fox said to the host : " Give us two good rooms, one for Mr. Pinocchio, and the other for me and my companion. We will snatch a little sleep before we leave. Remember, however, that at midnight we wish to be called to continue our journey."

" Yes, gentlemen," answered the host, and he winked at

the Fox and the Cat, as much as to say : " I know what you are up to. We understand one another ! "

No sooner had Pinocchio got into bed than he fell asleep at once and began to dream.

After some time he was suddenly wakened by three violent blows on the door of his room. It was the host who had come to tell him that midnight had struck.

" Are my companions ready ? " asked the puppet.

" Ready ! Why, they left two hours ago."

" Why were they in such a hurry ? "

" Because the Cat had received a message to say that her eldest kitten was ill with chilblains."

" Did they pay for the supper ? "

" What are you thinking of ? They are much too well educated to dream of offering such an insult to a gentleman like you."

" What a pity ! It is an insult that would have given me so much pleasure ! " said Pinocchio, scratching his head. He then asked : " And where did my good friends say they would wait for me ? "

" At the Field of miracles, to-morrow morning at day-break."

Pinocchio paid a sovereign for his supper and that of his companions, and then left.

Outside the inn it was so pitch dark that he had almost to grope his way.

As he was walking along he saw a little insect shining dimly on the trunk of a tree, like a night-light in a lamp of transparent china.

" Who are you ? " asked Pinocchio.

" I am the ghost of the Talking-cricket," answered the insect in a low voice, so weak and faint that it seemed to come from the other world. " I want to give you some advice. Go back, and take the four sovereigns that you have left to your poor father, who is weeping and in despair because you have never returned to him."

" By to-morrow my papa will be a gentleman, for these four sovereigns will have become two thousand."

" Don't trust, my boy, to those who promise to make you rich in a day. Usually they are either mad or rogues ! Give ear to me, and go back."

" On the contrary, I am determined to go on."

" Remember that boys who will have their own way, sooner or later repent it."

" Always the same stories. Good-night, Cricket."

" Good-night, Pinocchio, and may Heaven preserve you from dangers and from assassins."

No sooner had he said these words than the Talking-cricket vanished suddenly like a light that has been blown out, and the road became darker than ever.

" Really," said the puppet to himself as he resumed his journey, " how unfortunate we poor boys are. Everybody scolds us, everybody admonishes us, everybody gives us good advice."

But Pinocchio had not time to finish his reasoning, for he heard a slight rustle of leaves behind him. He turned to look, and saw in the gloom two evil-looking black figures completely enveloped in charcoal sacks. They were running after him on tiptoe, and making great leaps like two phantoms.

Not knowing where to hide his gold pieces he put them in his mouth precisely under his tongue. Then he tried to escape. But he had not gone a step when he felt himself seized by the arm, and heard two horrid sepulchral voices saying to him :

" Your money or your life ! "

Pinocchio, not being able to answer in words, owing
to the money that was in his mouth, made a thousand low
bows and a thousand pantomimes.   He tried thus to make
the two muffled figures, whose eyes were only visible
through the holes in their sacks, understand that he was a
poor puppet, and that he had not as much as a false farthing
in his pocket.

" Come now !   Less nonsense and out with the money ! "
cried the two brigands threateningly.

And the puppet made a gesture with his hands to
signify : " I have got none."

" Deliver up your money or you are dead," said the
tallest of the brigands.

" Dead ! " repeated the other.

" And after we have killed you, we will also kill your
father."

" Also your father ! "

" No, no, no, not my poor papa ! " cried Pinocchio
in a despairing tone ; and as he said it, the sovereigns
clinked in his mouth.

" Ah ! you rascal !   Then you have hidden your money
under your tongue !   Spit it out at once ! "

But Pinocchio was obdurate.

" Ah ! you pretend to be deaf, do you ? Wait a moment,
leave it to us to find a means to make you spit it out."

And one of them seized the puppet by the end of his
nose, and the other took him by the chin, and began to
pull them brutally, the one up and the other down, tc
constrain him to open his mouth. But it was all to no
purpose. Pinocchio's mouth seemed to be nailed and
riveted together.

Then the shorter assassin drew out an ugly knife and
tried to force it between his lips like a lever or chisel.

But Pinocchio, as quick as lightning, caught his hand. Imagine his astonishment when instead of a hand he perceived that it was a cat's paw. He used his nails to such purpose that he succeeded in liberating himself, and jumping the hedge, began to fly across country. The assassins ran after him like two dogs chasing a hare.

The day began to break and they were still pursuing him. Suddenly Pinocchio found his way barred by a wide deep ditch full of dirty water the colour of coffee. What was he to do? "One! two! three!" cried the puppet, and making a rush he sprang to the other side. The assassins also jumped, but not having measured the distance properly—splash, splash! . . . they fell into the very middle of the ditch. Pinocchio, who heard the plunge and the splashing of the water, shouted out, laughing, and without stopping:

"A fine bath to you, gentlemen assassins."

And he felt convinced that they were drowned, when, turning to look, he perceived that on the contrary they were both running after him, still enveloped in their sacks, with the water dripping from them as if they had been two hollow baskets.

At this sight the puppet's courage failed him, and he was on the point of throwing himself on the ground and giving himself over for lost.

"If I had only breath to reach that house," he said to himself, "perhaps I should be saved." And without delaying an instant, he recommenced running for his life through the wood, and the assassins after him. At last he arrived quite breathless at the door of the house, and knocked with great violence, for he heard the sound of steps approaching him, and the heavy panting of his persecutors. No one answered.

He began in desperation to kick and pummel the door with all his might. The window then opened and a beautiful Child appeared at it. She had blue hair and a face as white as a waxen image ; her eyes were closed and her hands were crossed on her breast. Without moving her lips in the least, she said in a voice that seemed to come from the other world : " In this house there is no one. They are all dead."

" Then at least open the door for me yourself," shouted Pinocchio.

" I am dead also."

Having said this she immediately disappeared, and the window was closed again without the slightest noise.

" Oh ! beautiful Child with blue hair," cried Pinocchio, " open the door for pity's sake ! Have compassion on a poor boy pursued by assas . . ."

But he could not finish the word, for he felt himself seized by the collar, and the same two horrible voices said to him threateningly : " You shall not escape from us again ! "

The puppet was taken with such a violent fit of trembling that the joints of his wooden legs began to creak and the sovereigns hidden under his tongue to clink.

" Now then," demanded the assassins, " will you open your mouth, yes or no ? Ah ! no answer ? . . ." And drawing out two long horrid knives as sharp as razors, clash . . . they attempted to stab him twice. But the puppet, luckily for him, was made of very hard wood ; the knives therefore broke into a thousand pieces, and the assassins were left with the handles in their hands staring at each other.

" I see what we must do," said one of them. " He must be hung ! let us hang him ! "

" Let us hang him ! " repeated the other.

Without loss of time they tied his arms behind him, passed a running noose round his throat, and then hung him to the branch of a tree called the Big Oak.

" Good-bye till to-morrow.   Let us hope that when we return you will be polite enough to allow yourself to be found quite dead, and with your mouth wide open."   And they walked off.

In the meantime a tempestuous northerly wind began to blow and roar, and it beat the poor puppet as he hung from side to side, making him swing violently like the clapper of a bell ringing for a wedding.   And the swinging gave him atrocious spasms, and the running noose, becoming still tighter round his throat, took away his breath. Little by little his eyes began to grow dim, but although he felt that death was near he still continued to hope that some charitable person would come to his assistance before it was too late.   But when, after waiting and waiting, he found that no one came, he remembered his poor father, and thinking he was dying . . . he stammered out : " Oh, papa ! papa ! if only you were here ! "

His breath failed him and he could say no more.   He shut his eyes, opened his mouth, stretched his legs, gave a long shudder, and hung stiff and insensible.

VI

THE beautiful Child with blue hair came again to the window. When she saw the unhappy puppet hanging by his throat, and dancing up and down in the gusts of the north wind, she was moved by compassion. Striking her hands together she made three little claps. At this signal a large Falcon flew on to the window-sill.

"What are your orders, gracious Fairy?" he asked, inclining his beak in sign of reverence—for I must tell you that the Child with blue hair was no more and no less than a beautiful Fairy, who for more than a thousand years had lived in the wood.

"Fly at once: with your strong beak break the knot that keeps that puppet suspended in the air, and lay him gently on the grass at the foot of the tree."

The Falcon flew away, and after two minutes he returned, saying: "I have done as you commanded. To see him he appeared dead, but he cannot really be quite dead, for I had no sooner loosened the running noose that tightened his throat than, giving a sigh, he muttered in a faint voice: 'Now I feel better! . . .'"

The Fairy then striking her hands together made two little claps, and a magnificent Poodle appeared, walking upright on his hind-legs.

He was in the full-dress livery of a coachman.

" Be quick, Medoro," said the Fairy to the Poodle. " Bring the poor puppet here to me."

Shortly afterwards a beautiful little carriage came out of the coach-house, and the Poodle, seated on the coach-box, cracked his whip from side to side like a driver.

When the carriage returned, the Fairy took the poor puppet in her arms, and carried him into a little room that was wainscotted with mother-of-pearl, and sent at once to summon the most famous doctors in the neighbourhood.

The doctors came immediately one after the other : namely a Crow, an Owl, and a Talking-cricket.

" I wish to know from you gentlemen," said the Fairy, turning to the three doctors who were assembled round Pinocchio's bed—" I wish to know from you gentlemen, if this unfortunate puppet is alive or dead ! . . ."

At this request the Crow, advancing first, felt Pinocchio's pulse ; he then felt his nose, and then the little toe of his foot : and having done this carefully, he pronounced solemnly the following words : " To my belief the puppet is already quite dead ; but if unfortunately he should not be dead, then it would be a sign that he is still alive ! "

" I regret," said the Owl, " to be obliged to contradict the Crow, my illustrious friend and colleague ; but in my opinion the puppet is still alive : but if unfortunately he should not be alive, then it would be a sign that he is dead indeed ! "

" And you—have you nothing to say ? " asked the Fairy of the Talking-cricket.

" In my opinion the wisest thing a prudent doctor can do, when he does not know what he is talking about, is to be silent. For the rest, that puppet there has a face that is not new to me. I have known him for some time ! . . ."

Pinocchio, who up to that moment had lain immovable, like a real piece of wood, was seized with a fit of convulsive trembling that shook the whole bed.

" That puppet there," continued the Talking-cricket, " is a confirmed rogue. . . ."

Pinocchio opened his eyes, but shut them again immediately.

" He is a ragamuffin, a do-nothing, a vagabond. . . ."

Pinocchio hid his face beneath the clothes.

" That puppet there is a disobedient son who will make his poor father die of a broken heart ! . . ."

At that instant a suffocated sound of sobs and crying was heard in the room. Imagine everybody's astonishment when, having raised the sheets a little, it was discovered that the sounds came from Pinocchio.

" When the dead person cries, it is a sign that he is on the road to get well," said the Crow solemnly.

" I grieve to contradict my illustrious friend and colleague," added the Owl ; " but for me, when the dead person cries, it is a sign that he is sorry to die."

As soon as the three doctors had left the room the Fairy approached Pinocchio, and having touched his forehead she perceived that he was in a high fever.

She therefore dissolved a certain white powder in half a tumbler of water, and offering it to the puppet she said to him lovingly : " Drink it, and in a few days you will be cured."

Pinocchio looked at the tumbler, made a wry face, and then asked in a plaintive voice : " Is it sweet or bitter ? "

" It is bitter, but it will do you good."

" If it is bitter, I will not take it."

" Listen to me : drink it."

" I don't like anything bitter."

" Drink it, and when you have drunk it I will give you a lump of sugar to take away the taste."

" Where is the lump of sugar ? "

" Here it is," said the Fairy, taking a piece from a gold sugar-basin.

" Give me first the lump of sugar, and then I will drink that bad bitter water. . . ."

" Do you promise me ? "

" Yes. . . ."

The Fairy gave him the sugar, and Pinocchio, having crunched it up and swallowed it in a second, said, licking his lips : " It would be a fine thing if sugar was medicine ! . . . I would take it every day."

" Now keep your promise and drink these few drops of water, which will restore you to health."

Pinocchio took the tumbler unwillingly in his hand and put the point of his nose to it : he then approached it to his lips : he then again put his nose to it, and at last said : " It is too bitter ! too bitter ! I cannot drink it."

" How can you tell that, when you have not even tasted it ? "

" I can imagine it ! I know it from the smell. I want first another lump of sugar . . . and then I will drink it ! . . ."

The Fairy then, with all the patience of a good mamma, put another lump of sugar in his mouth, and then again presented the tumbler to him.

" I cannot drink it so ! " said the puppet, making a thousand grimaces.

" Why ? "

" Because that pillow that is down there on my feet bothers me."

The Fairy removed the pillow.

" The door of the room, which is half open, bothers me."
The Fairy went and closed the door.

" In short," cried Pinocchio, bursting into tears, " I
will not drink that bitter water—no, no, no ! . . ."

" My boy, you will repent it. . . ."

" I don't care. . . ."

" Your illness is serious. . . ."

" I don't care. . . ."

" The fever in a few hours will carry you into the other
world. . . ."

" I don't care. . . ."

" Are you not afraid of death ? "

" I am not in the least afraid ! . . . I would rather die
than drink that bitter medicine."

At that moment the door of the room flew open, and
four rabbits as black as ink entered carrying on their
shoulders a little bier.

" What do you want with me ? " cried Pinocchio, sitting
up in bed in a great fright.

" We are come to take you," said the biggest rabbit.

" To take me ? . . . But I am not yet dead ! . . ."

" No, not yet : but you have only a few minutes to live,
as you have refused the medicine that would have cured
you of the fever."

" Oh, Fairy, Fairy ! " the puppet then began to scream,
" give me the tumbler at once . . . be quick, for pity's
sake, for I will not die—no . . . I will not die. . . ."

And taking the tumbler in both hands he emptied it at a
draught.

" We must have patience ! " said the rabbits ; " this
time we have made our journey in vain." And taking the
little bier again on their shoulders they left the room,
grumbling and murmuring between their teeth.

In fact, a few minutes afterwards Pinocchio jumped down from the bed quite well.

The Fairy, seeing him running and rushing about the room as gay and as lively as a young cock, said to him : " Then my medicine has really done you good ? "

" Good, I should think so ! It has restored me to life ! . . ."

" Then why on earth did you require so much persuasion to take it ? "

" Because you see that we boys are all like that ! We are more afraid of medicine than of the illness."

" Disgraceful ! Boys ought to know that a good remedy taken in time may save them from a serious illness, and perhaps even from death. . . ."

" Oh ! but another time I shall not require so much persuasion. I shall remember those black rabbits with the bier on their shoulders . . . and then I shall immediately take the tumbler in my hand, and down it will go ! . . ."

" And the four pieces — where have you put them ? " asked the Fairy.

" I have lost them ! " said Pinocchio ; but he was telling a lie, for he had them in his pocket.

He had scarcely told the lie when his nose, which was already long, grew at once two fingers longer.

" And where did you lose them ? "

" In the wood near here."

At this second lie his nose went on growing.

" If you have lost them in the wood near here," said the Fairy, " we will look for them, and we shall find them : because everything that is lost in that wood is always found."

" Ah ! now I remember all about it," replied the puppet, getting quite confused ; " I didn't lose the four gold pieces, I swallowed them whilst I was drinking your medicine."

At this third lie his nose grew to such an extraordinary length that poor Pinocchio could not move in any direction. If he turned to one side he struck his nose against the bed or the window-panes, if he turned to the other he struck it against the walls or the door, if he raised his head a little he ran the risk of sticking it into one of the Fairy's eyes. And the Fairy looked at him and laughed.

" What are you laughing at ? " asked the puppet, very confused and anxious at finding his nose growing so prodigiously.

" I am laughing at the lie you have told."

" And how can you possibly know that I have told a lie ? "

" Lies, my dear boy, are found out immediately, because they are of two sorts. There are lies that have short legs, and lies that have long noses. Your lie, as it happens, is one of those that have a long nose."

Pinocchio, not knowing where to hide himself for shame, tried to run out of the room ; but he did not succeed, for his nose had increased so much that it could no longer pass through the door.

The Fairy allowed the puppet to cry and to roar for a good half-hour over his nose. But when she saw him disfigured, and his eyes swollen from weeping, she felt compassion for him. She therefore beat her hands together, when a thousand large Woodpeckers flew in at the window. They immediately perched on Pinocchio's nose, and began to peck at it with such zeal that in a few minutes it was reduced to its usual dimensions.

" What a good Fairy you are," said the puppet, drying his eyes, " and how much I love you ! "

" I love you also," answered the Fairy ; " and if you will

remain with me, you shall be my little brother and I will be your good little sister. . . ."

" I would remain willingly . . . but my poor papa ? "

" I have thought of everything. I have already let your father know, and he will be here to-night."

" Really ? " shouted Pinocchio, jumping for joy. " Then, little Fairy, if you consent, I should like to go and meet him."

" Go, then, but be careful not to lose yourself. Take the road through the wood and I am sure that you will meet him."

Pinocchio set out ; and as soon as he was in the wood he began to run like a kid. But when he had reached a certain spot, he thought that he heard people amongst the bushes. In fact, two persons came out on to the road . . . his two travelling companions, the Fox and the Cat.

" Why, here is our dear Pinocchio ! " cried the Fox, embracing him. " How come you to be here ? "

" How come you to be here ? " repeated the Cat.

" It is a long story," answered the puppet. " But do you know that when you left me alone at the inn, I met with assassins on the road. . . ."

" Assassins ! . . . And what did they want ? "

" They wanted to rob me of my gold pieces."

" Villains ! . . ." said the Fox.

" Infamous villains ! " repeated the Cat.

" And now, what are you doing here ? " asked the Fox of the Puppet.

" I am waiting for my papa."

" And your gold pieces ? "

" I have got them in my pocket, all but one that I spent at the inn of the Red Craw-fish."

" And to think that, instead of four pieces, by to-morrow

they might become one or two thousand ! Why do you not listen to my advice ? why will you not go and bury them in the Field of miracles ? "

" How far off is the Field of miracles ? "

" Not two miles. Will you come with us ? In half an hour you will be there. You can bury your money at once, and in a few minutes you will collect two thousand, and this evening you will return with your pockets full. Will you come with us ? "

Pinocchio thought of the good Fairy, old Geppetto, and the warnings of the Talking-cricket, and he hesitated a little before answering. He ended by giving his head a little shake, and saying to the Fox and the Cat : " Let us go : I will come with you."

After having walked half the day they reached a solitary field which to look at resembled all other fields.

" We are arrived," said the Fox to the puppet. " Now stoop down and dig with your hands a little hole in the ground and put your gold pieces into it."

Pinocchio dug a hole, put into it the four gold pieces that he had left, and then filled up the hole with a little earth.

" Now, then," said the Fox, " go to that canal close to us, fetch a can of water, and water the ground."

Pinocchio went to the canal, and as he had no can he took off one of his old shoes, and filling it with water he watered the ground over the hole.

He then asked : " Is there anything else to be done ? "

" Nothing else," answered the Fox. " We can now go away. You can return in about twenty minutes, and you will find a shrub already pushing through the ground, with its branches quite loaded with money."

The poor puppet thanked the Fox and the Cat a thousand times, and promised them a beautiful present.

" We wish for no presents," answered the two rascals. " It is enough for us to have taught you the way to enrich yourself without undergoing hard work."

VII

THE puppet returned to the town and began to count the minutes one by one ; and when he thought that it must be time he took the road leading to the Field of miracles.

Whilst he was building castles in the air he arrived in the neighbourhood of the field, and stopped to look if by chance he could perceive a tree with its branches laden with money : but he saw nothing. He advanced another hundred steps — nothing : he entered the field . . . he went right up to the little hole where he had buried his sovereigns—and nothing. He then became very thoughtful, and forgetting the rules of society and good manners he took his hands out of his pockets and gave his head a long scratch.

Pinocchio began with his hands and nails to dig up the earth that he had watered : but the money was no longer there.

He rushed back and went at once to the Courts of Justice to denounce the two knaves who had robbed him to the judge.

Pinocchio related all the particulars of the fraud.

The judge listened with great benignity; took a lively interest in the story; was much touched and moved; and when the puppet had nothing further to say he stretched out his hand and rang a bell.

At this summons two mastiffs immediately appeared dressed as gendarmes. The judge then, pointing to Pinocchio, said to them: " That poor devil has been robbed of four gold pieces; take him up, and put him immediately into prison."

The puppet on hearing this unexpected sentence tried to protest; but the gendarmes stopped his mouth and carried him off to the lock-up.

And there he remained for four months; and he would have remained longer still if a fortunate chance had not released him. For the young Emperor who reigned over the town, having won a splendid victory over his enemies, ordered great public rejoicings. There were illuminations, and fire-works, and as a further sign of triumph he commanded that all the prisoners should be liberated.

" If the others are to be let out of prison, I will go also," said Pinocchio to the jailer.

" No, not you," said the jailer, " because you do not belong to the fortunate class."

" I beg your pardon," replied Pinocchio, " I am also a criminal."

" In that case you are perfectly right," said the jailer; and taking off his hat and bowing to him respectfully he opened the prison doors and let him escape.

You can imagine Pinocchio's joy when he found himself free. Without stopping to take breath he immediately left the town and took the road that led to the Fairy's house.

But before long he began to suffer so dreadfully from hunger that he could not bear it, and he jumped into a field by the wayside intending to pick some bunches of muscatel grapes. Oh, that he had never done it !

He had scarcely reached the vines when crac . . . his legs were caught between two cutting iron bars, and he became so giddy with pain that stars of every colour danced before his eyes.

The poor puppet had been taken in a trap put there to capture some big polecats who were the scourge of the poultry-yards in the neighbourhood. Pinocchio, as you can imagine, began to cry and scream : but his tears and groans were useless, for there was not a house to be seen, and not a living soul passed down the road.

At last night came on. Partly from the pain of the trap that cut his legs, and a little from fear at finding himself alone in the dark in the midst of the fields, the puppet was on the point of fainting. Just at that moment he saw a Firefly flitting over his head. He called to it and said ; " Oh, little Firefly, will you have pity on me and liberate me from this torture ɿ "

" Poor boy ! " said the Firefly, stopping and looking at him with compassion, " but how could your legs have been caught by those sharp irons ɿ "

" I came into the field to pick two bunches of these muscatel grapes, and . . ."

" But were the grapes yours ɿ "

" No. . . ."

" Then who taught you to carry off other people's property ɿ "

" I was so hungry. . . ."

" Hunger, my boy, is not a good reason for appropriating what does not belong to us. . . ."

" That is true, that is true ! " said Pinocchio, crying. " I will never do it again."

At this moment their conversation was interrupted by a slight sound of approaching footsteps. It was the owner of the field coming on tiptoe to see if one of the polecats that ate his chickens during the night had been caught in his trap. His astonishment was great when, having brought out his lantern from under his coat, he perceived that instead of a polecat a boy had been taken.

" Ah, little thief ! " said the angry peasant, " then it is you who carry off my chickens ? "

" No, it is not I ; indeed it is not ! " cried Pinocchio, sobbing. " I only came into the field to take two bunches of grapes ! . . ."

" He who steals grapes is quite capable of stealing chickens. Leave it to me, I will give you a lesson that you will not forget in a hurry."

Opening the trap he seized the puppet by the collar, and carried him to his house as if he had been a young lamb.

When he reached the yard in front of the house he threw him roughly on the ground, and putting his foot on his neck he said to him : " It is late, and I want to go to bed ; we will settle our accounts to-morrow. In the meanwhile, as the dog who kept guard at night died to-day, you shall take his place at once. You shall be my watch-dog."

And taking a great collar covered with brass knobs he strapped it tightly round his throat that he might not be able to draw his head out of it. A heavy chain attached to the collar was fastened to the wall.

" If it should rain to-night," he then said to him, " you can go and lie down in the kennel ; the straw that has served as a bed for my poor dog for the last four years is still there. If unfortunately robbers should come, remember to keep your ears pricked and to bark."

After giving him this last injunction the man went into the house, shut the door, and put up the chain.

Poor Pinocchio remained lying on the ground more dead than alive from the effects of cold, hunger, and fear. From time to time he put his hands angrily to the collar that tightened his throat and said, crying : " It serves me right ! . . . Decidedly it serves me right ! I was determined to be a vagabond and a good-for-nothing. . . . I would listen to bad companions, and that is why I always meet with misfortunes. If I had been a good little boy as so many are ; if I had been willing to learn and to work ; if I had remained at home with my poor papa, I should not now be in the midst of the fields and obliged to be the watch-dog to a peasant's house. Oh, if I could be born again ! But now it is too late, and I must have patience ! "

Relieved by this little outburst, which came straight from his heart, he went into the dog-kennel and fell asleep.

He had been sleeping heavily for about two hours when, towards midnight, he was roused by a whispering of strange voices that seemed to come from the courtyard. Putting the point of his nose out of the kennel he saw four little beasts with dark fur, that looked like cats, standing consulting together. But they were not cats ; they were polecats—carnivorous little animals, especially greedy for eggs and young chickens. One of the polecats, leaving his companions, came to the opening of the kennel and said in a low voice :

" Good evening, Melampo."

" My name is not Melampo," answered the puppet.

" Oh ! then who are you ? "

" I am Pinocchio."

" And what are you doing here ? "

" I am acting as watch-dog."

" Then where is Melampo ?   Where is the old dog who lived in this kennel ? "

" He died this morning."

" Is he dead ?   Poor beast !   He was so good.   But judging you by your face I should say that you were also a good dog."

" I beg your pardon, I am not a dog."

" Not a dog ?   Then what are you ? "

" I am a puppet."

" And you are acting as watch-dog ? "

" That is only too true—as a punishment."

" Well, then, I will offer you the same conditions that we made with the deceased Melampo, and I am sure you will be satisfied with them."

" What are these conditions ? "

" One night in every week you are to permit us to visit this poultry-yard as we have hitherto done, and to carry off eight chickens.   Of these chickens seven are to be eaten by us, and one we will give to you, on the express understanding, however, that you pretend to be asleep, and that it never enters your head to bark and to wake the peasant."

" Did Melampo act in this manner ? " asked Pinocchio.

" Certainly, and we were always on the best terms with him.   Sleep quietly, and rest assured that before we go we will leave by the kennel a beautiful chicken ready plucked for your breakfast to-morrow.   Have we understood each other clearly ? "

" Only too clearly ! . . ." answered Pinocchio, and he shook his head threateningly as much as to say : " You shall hear of this shortly ! "

The four polecats thinking themselves safe repaired to the poultry-yard, which was close to the kennel, and having opened the wooden gate with their teeth and claws, they slipped in one by one. But they had only just passed through when they heard the gate shut behind them with great violence.

It was Pinocchio who had shut it ; and for greater security he put a large stone against it to keep it closed. He then began to bark, and he barked exactly like a watch-dog : bow - bow, bow - wow. Hearing the barking the peasant jumped out of bed, and taking his gun he came to the window and asked : " What is the matter ? "

" There are robbers ! " answered Pinocchio.

" Where are they ? "

" In the poultry-yard."

" I will come down directly."

In fact in less time than it takes to say Amen, the peasant came down. He rushed into the poultry-yard, caught the polecats, and having put them into a sack, he said to them in a tone of great satisfaction :

" At last you have fallen into my hands ! I might punish you, but I am not so cruel. I will content myself instead by carrying you in the morning to the innkeeper of the neighbouring village, who will skin and cook you as hares with a sweet and sour sauce. It is an honour that you don't deserve, but generous people like me don't consider such trifles ! . . ."

He then approached Pinocchio and began to caress him, and amongst other things he asked him : " How did you manage to discover the four thieves ? To think that Melampo, my faithful Melampo, never found out anything ! . . ."

The puppet might then have told him the whole story ; he might have informed him of the disgraceful conditions that had been made between the dog and the polecats ;

but he remembered that the dog was dead, and he thought to himself : " What is the good of accusing the dead ? . . . The dead are dead, and the best thing to be done is to leave them in peace ! . . ."

" When the thieves got into the yard were you asleep or awake ? " the peasant went on to ask him.

" I was asleep," answered Pinocchio, " but the polecats woke me with their chatter, and one of them came to the kennel and said to me : ' If you promise not to bark and not to wake the master, we will make you a present of a fine chicken ready plucked ! . . .' To think that they should have had the audacity to make such a proposal to me ! For although I am a puppet, possessing perhaps nearly all the faults in the world, there is one that I certainly will never be guilty of, that of making terms with, and sharing in the gains of, dishonest people ! "

" Well said, my boy ! " cried the peasant, slapping him on the shoulder. " Such sentiments do you honour : and as a proof of my gratitude I will at once set you at liberty, and you may return home."

And he removed the dog's collar.

As soon as Pinocchio was released from the heavy and humiliating weight of the dog-collar he started off across the fields, and never stopped until he had reached the high road that led to the Fairy's house. There he turned and looked down into the plain beneath. He could see distinctly with his naked eye the wood where he had been so unfortunate as to meet with the Fox and the Cat ; he could see amongst the trees the top of the Big Oak to which he had been hung; but although he looked in every direction, the little house belonging to the beautiful Child with the blue hair was nowhere visible.

Seized with a sad presentiment he began to run with all

the strength he had left, and in a few minutes he reached the field where the little white house had once stood. He saw a marble stone, on which were engraved these sad words :

HERE LIES

THE CHILD WITH THE BLUE HAIR,

WHO DIED FROM SORROW

BECAUSE SHE WAS ABANDONED BY HER

LITTLE BROTHER PINOCCHIO.

I leave you to imagine the puppet's feelings when he had with difficulty spelt out this epitaph. He fell with his face on the ground and, covering the tombstone with a thousand kisses, burst into an agony of tears. He cried all night, and when morning came he was still crying although he had no tears left.

And as he wept he said : " Oh, little Fairy, why did you die ? Why did not I die instead of you, I who am so wicked, whilst you were so good ? . . . And my papa ? Where can he be ? Oh, little Fairy, tell me where I can find him, for I want to remain with him always and never to leave him again, never again ! . . . Oh, little Fairy, tell me that it is not true that you are dead ! . . . If you really love me . . . if you really love your little brother, come to life again . . . come to life as you were before ! . . . What can I do here alone in the world ? Now that I have lost you and my papa, who will give me food ? Where shall I go to sleep at night ? Oh, it would be better, a hundred times better, that I should die also ! Yes, I want to die ! . . ."

And in his despair he tried to tear his hair ; but his hair

being made of wood, he could not even have the satisfaction of sticking his fingers into it.

Just then a large Pigeon flew over his head, and stopping with distended wings called down to him from a great height : " Tell me, child, what are you doing there ? "

" Don't you see ? I am crying ! " said Pinocchio, raising his head towards the voice and rubbing his eyes with his jacket.

" Tell me," continued the Pigeon, " amongst your companions, do you happen to know a puppet who is called Pinocchio ? "

" Pinocchio ? . . . Did you say Pinocchio ? " repeated the puppet, jumping quickly to his feet. " I am Pinocchio ! "

The Pigeon at this answer descended rapidly to the ground. He was larger than a turkey.

" Do you also know Geppetto ? " he asked.

" Do I know him ! He is my poor papa ! Has he spoken to you of me ? Will you take me to him ? Answer me for pity's sake : is he still alive ? "

" I left him three days ago on the sea-shore."

" What was he doing ? "

" He was building a little boat for himself, to cross the ocean. For more than three months that poor man has been going all round the world looking for you. He has now taken it into his head to go to the distant countries of the new world in search of you."

" How far is it from here to the shore ? " asked Pinocchio breathlessly.

" More than six hundred miles."

" Six hundred miles ? Oh, beautiful Pigeon, what a fine thing it would be to have your wings ! . . ."

" If you wish to go, I will carry you there."

" How ? "

" Astride on my back.   Do you weigh much ? "

" I weigh next to nothing.   I am as light as a feather."

And without waiting for more, Pinocchio jumped on the Pigeon's back, and putting a leg on each side of him he exclaimed joyfully : " Gallop, gallop, my little horse, for I am anxious to arrive quickly ! . . ."

The Pigeon took flight, and in a few minutes had soared so high that they almost touched the clouds. Finding himself at such an immense height the puppet had the curiosity to turn and look down ; but his head spun round, and he became so frightened, that to save himself from the danger of falling he wound his arms tightly round the neck of his feathered steed.

They flew all day.   Towards evening the Pigeon said : " I am very thirsty ! "

" And I am very hungry ! " rejoined Pinocchio.

" Let us stop at that dovecot for a few minutes ; and then we will continue our journey that we may reach the seashore by dawn to-morrow."

They went into a deserted dovecot, where they found nothing but a basin full of water and a basket full of vetch. The puppet had never in his life been able to eat vetch : according to him it made him sick.   That evening, however, he ate to repletion, and when he had nearly emptied the basket he turned to the Pigeon and said to him : " I never could have believed that vetch was so good ! "

" Be assured, my boy," replied the Pigeon, " that when hunger is real, and there is nothing else to eat, even vetch becomes delicious."

Having finished their little meal they recommenced their journey. The following morning they reached the seashore.

The Pigeon flew quickly away and disappeared. The shore was crowded with people who were looking out to sea, shouting and gesticulating.

" What has happened ? " asked Pinocchio of an old woman.

" A poor father who has lost his son has gone away in a boat to search for him on the other side of the water, and to-day the sea is tempestuous and the little boat is in danger of sinking."

" Where is the little boat ? "

" It is out there in a line with my finger," said the old woman, pointing to a little boat which, seen at that distance, looked like a nutshell with a very little man in it.

Pinocchio fixed his eyes on it, and after looking attentively he gave a piercing scream, crying : " It is my papa ! it is my papa ! "

The boat meanwhile, beaten by the fury of the waves, at one moment disappeared in the trough of the sea, and the next came again to the surface. Pinocchio, standing on the top of a high rock, kept calling to his father by name, and making every kind of signal to him with his hands, his handkerchief, and his cap. And although he was so far off, Geppetto appeared to recognise his son, for he also took off his cap and waved it, and tried by gestures to make him understand that he would have returned if it had been possible, but that the sea was so tempestuous that he could not use his oars or approach the shore. Suddenly a tremendous wave rose and the boat disappeared. They waited, hoping it would come again to the surface, but it was seen no more.

" Poor man ! " said the fishermen who were assembled on the shore, and murmuring a prayer they turned to go home.

Just then they heard a desperate cry, and looking back they saw a little boy who exclaimed, as he jumped from a rock into the sea : " I will save my papa ! "

Pinocchio, being made of wood, floated easily and he swam like a fish. At one moment they saw him disappear under the water, carried down by the fury of the waves ; and next he reappeared struggling with a leg or an arm. At last they lost sight of him, and he was seen no more.

" Poor boy ! " said the fishermen who were collected on the shore, and murmuring a prayer they returned home.

VIII

PINOCCHIO, hoping to be in time to help his father, swam the whole night.

And what a horrible night it was ! The rain came down in torrents, it hailed, the thunder was frightful, and the flashes of lightning made it as light as day.

Towards morning he saw a long strip of land not far off. It was an island in the midst of the sea. He tried his utmost to reach the shore : but it was all in vain. The waves knocked him about as if he had been a stick or a wisp of straw. At last a billow rolled up with such fury that he was lifted up and thrown violently far on to the sands.

He fell with such force that, as he struck the ground, his ribs and all his joints cracked.

Little by little the sky cleared, the sun shone out, and the sea became as quiet and smooth as oil. The puppet put his clothes in the sun to dry, and began to look in every direction in hopes of seeing on the vast expanse of water a little boat with a little man in it. But he could see nothing but the sky, and the sea, and the sail of some ship, but so far away that it seemed no bigger than a fly.

This idea of finding himself alone, alone, all alone, in the midst of this great uninhabited country, made him so melancholy that he was just beginning to cry. But at that moment, at a short distance from the shore, he saw a big fish swimming by ; it was going quietly on its own business with its head out of the water.

Not knowing its name the puppet called to it in a loud voice to make himself heard : " Eh, Sir fish, will you permit me a word with you ? "

" Two if you like," answered the fish, who was a Dolphin, and very polite.

" Have you by chance met a little boat with my papa in it ? "

" And who is your papa ? "

" He is the best papa in the world, whilst it would be difficult to find a worse son than I am."

" During the terrible storm last night," answered the Dolphin, " the little boat must have gone to the bottom."

" And my papa ? "

" He must have been swallowed by the terrible Dog-fish."

" Is this Dog-fish very big ? " asked Pinocchio, who was already beginning to quake with fear.

" Big ! . . ." replied the Dolphin. " I need only tell you that he is bigger than a five-storied house, and that his mouth is so enormous and so deep that a railway train could pass easily down his throat."

" Mercy upon us ! " exclaimed the terrified puppet ; and putting on his clothes with the greatest haste he said to the Dolphin : " Good-bye, Sir fish : excuse the trouble I have given you, and many thanks for your politeness."

He then began to walk fast—so fast, indeed, that he was almost running. And at the slightest noise he turned to look behind him, fearing that he might see the terrible Dog-fish with a railway train in its mouth following him. After a walk of half an hour he reached a little village called " The village of the Industrious Bees." The road was alive with people running here and there to attend to their business : all were at work, all had something to do.

" Ah ! " said that lazy Pinocchio at once, " I see that this village will never suit me ! "

In the meanwhile he was tormented by hunger, for he had eaten nothing for twenty-four hours—not even vetch.

There were only two ways by which he could obtain food—either by asking for a little work, or by begging for a halfpenny or for a mouthful of bread.   He was ashamed to beg, for his father had always preached to him that no one had a right to beg except the aged and the infirm.   It is the duty of every one else to work ; and if they will not work, so much the worse for them if they suffer from hunger.

At that moment a man came down the road, tired and panting for breath.   He was dragging alone, with fatigue and difficulty, two carts full of charcoal.

Pinocchio, judging by his face that he was a kind man, approached him, and casting down his eyes with shame he said to him in a low voice : " Would you have the charity to give me a halfpenny, for I am dying of hunger ? "

" You shall have not only a halfpenny," said the man, " but I will give you twopence, provided that you help me to drag home these two carts of charcoal."

" I am surprised at you ! " answered the puppet in a tone of offence.   " Let me tell you that I am not accustomed to do the work of a donkey : I have never drawn a cart ! . . ."

" So much the better for you," answered the man. " Then, my boy, if you are really dying of hunger, eat two fine slices of your pride, and be careful not to get an indigestion."

A few minutes afterwards a mason passed down the road carrying on his shoulders a basket of lime.

" Would you have the charity, good man, to give a halfpenny to a poor boy who is yawning for want of food ? "

" Willingly," answered the man. " Come with me and carry the lime, and instead of a halfpenny I will give you five."

" But the lime is heavy," objected Pinocchio, " and I don't want to tire myself."

" If you don't want to tire yourself, then, my boy, amuse yourself with yawning, and much good may it do you."

In less than half an hour twenty other people went by ; and Pinocchio asked charity of them all, but they all answered : " Are you not ashamed to beg ? Instead of idling about the roads, go and look for a little work and learn to earn your bread."

At last a nice little woman carrying two cans of water came by.

" Will you let me drink a little water out of your can ? " asked Pinocchio, who was burning with thirst.

" Drink, my boy, if you wish it ! " said the little woman, setting down the two cans.

Pinocchio drank like a fish, and as he dried his mouth he mumbled : " I have quenched my thirst. If I could only appease my hunger ! . . ."

The good woman hearing these words said at once : " If you will help me to carry home these two cans of water, I will give you a fine piece of bread."

Pinocchio looked at the can and answered neither yes nor no.

" And besides the bread you shall have a nice dish of cauliflower dressed with oil and vinegar," added the good woman.

Pinocchio gave another look at the can, and answered neither yes nor no.

" And after the cauliflower, I will give you a beautiful bonbon full of syrup."

The temptation of this last dainty was so great that Pinocchio could resist no longer, and with an air of decision he said : " I will carry the can to your house."

The can was heavy, and the puppet not being strong enough to carry it in his hand, had to carry it on his head. When they reached the house the good little woman made Pinocchio sit down at a small table already laid, and she placed before him the bread, the cauliflower, and the bonbon. Pinocchio did not eat, he devoured.

When his ravenous hunger was somewhat appeased he raised his head to thank his benefactress ; but he had no sooner looked at her than he gave a prolonged Oh-h-h ! of astonishment, and continued staring at her, with wide open eyes, his fork in the air, and his mouth full of bread and cauliflower, as if he had been bewitched.

" What has surprised you so much ? " asked the good woman, laughing.

" It is . . ." answered the puppet, " it is . . . it is . . . that you are like . . . that you remind me . . . yes, yes, yes, the same voice . . . the same eyes . . . the same hair . . . yes, yes, yes . . . you also have blue hair . . . as she had. . . . Oh, little Fairy ! . . . tell me that it is you, really you ! . . . Do not make me cry any more ! If you knew . . . I have cried so much, I have suffered so much. . . ."

And throwing himself at her feet on the floor, Pinocchio embraced the knees of the mysterious little woman and began to cry bitterly.

At first the good little woman maintained that she was

not the little Fairy with blue hair; but seeing that she was found out, and not wishing to continue the comedy any longer, she ended by making herself known, and she said to Pinocchio :

" You little rogue ! how did you ever discover who I was ? "

" It was my great affection for you that told me."

" Do you remember ? You left me a child, and now that you have found me again I am a woman—a woman almost old enough to be your mamma."

" I am delighted at that, for now, instead of calling you little sister, I will call you mamma. I have wished for such a long time to have a mamma like other boys ! . . . . But how did you manage to grow so fast ? "

" That is a secret."

" Teach it to me, for I should also like to grow. Don't you see ? I always remain no bigger than a ninepin."

" But you cannot grow," replied the Fairy.

" Why ? "

" Because puppets never grow. They are born puppets, live puppets, and die puppets."

" Oh, I am sick of being a puppet ! " cried Pinocchio, giving himself a slap. " It is time that I became a man. . . ."

" And you will become one, if you know how to deserve it. . . ."

" Not really ? And what can I do to deserve it ? "

" A very easy thing : by learning to be a good boy."

" And you think I am not ? "

" You are quite the contrary. Good boys are obedient, and you . . ."

" And I never obey."

" Good boys like to learn and to work, and you . . ."

" And I instead lead an idle vagabond life the year through."

" Good boys always speak the truth. . . ."

" And I always tell lies."

" Good boys go willingly to school. . . ."

" And school gives me pain all over my body. But from to-day I will change my life."

" Do you promise me ? "

" I promise you. I will become a good little boy, and I will be the consolation of my papa. . . . Where is my poor papa at this moment ? "

" I do not know."

" Shall I ever have the happiness of seeing him again and kissing him ? "

" I think so ; indeed I am sure of it."

At this answer Pinocchio was so delighted that he took the Fairy's hands and began to kiss them with such fervour that he seemed beside himself. Then raising his face and looking at her lovingly, he asked : " Tell me, little mamma : then it was not true that you were dead ? "

" It seems not," said the Fairy, smiling.

" If you only knew the sorrow I felt and the tightening of my throat when I read, ' here lies . . .' "

" I know it, and it is on that account that I have forgiven you. I saw from the sincerity of your grief that you had a good heart ; and when boys have good hearts, even if they are scamps and have got bad habits, there is always something to hope for : that is, there is always hope that they will turn to better ways. That is why I came to look for you here. I will be your mamma. . . ."

" Oh, how delightful ! " shouted Pinocchio, jumping for joy.

" You must obey me and do everything that I bid you."

" Willingly, willingly, willingly ! "

" To-morrow," rejoined the Fairy, " you will begin to go to school."

Pinocchio became at once a little less joyful.

" Then you must choose an art, or a trade, according to your own wishes."

Pinocchio became very grave.

" What are you muttering between your teeth ? " asked the Fairy in an angry voice.

" I was saying," moaned the puppet in a low voice, " that it seemed too late for me to go to school now. . . ."

" No, sir. Keep it in mind that it is never too late to learn and to instruct ourselves."

" But I do not wish to follow either an art or a trade."

" Why ? "

" Because it tires me to work."

" My boy," said the Fairy, " those who talk in that way end almost always either in prison or in the hospital. Let me tell you that every man, whether he is born rich or poor, is obliged to do something in this world. Sloth is a dreadful illness and must be cured at once, in childhood. When we are old it can never be cured."

Pinocchio was touched by these words, and lifting his head quickly he said to the Fairy : " I will study, I will work, I will do all that you tell me, for indeed I have become weary of being a puppet, and I wish at any price to become a boy. You promised me that I should, did you not ? "

" I did promise you, and it now depends upon yourself."

The following day Pinocchio went to school. Imagine the delight of all the little rogues when they saw a puppet walk into their school ! They set up a roar of laughter that never ended. They played him all sorts of tricks. One boy carried off his cap, another pulled his jacket behind ; one tried to give him a pair of inky mustachios just under his nose, and another attempted to tie strings to his feet and hands to make him dance.

For a short time Pinocchio pretended not to care, and got on as well as he could ; but at last, losing all patience, he turned to those who were teasing him most and making game of him, and said to them, looking very angry : "Beware, boys : I am not come here to be your buffoon. I respect others, and I intend to be respected."

This firmness acquired at once for Pinocchio the sympathy and the esteem of all the boys in the school. They all made friends with him and liked him heartily. Even the master praised him, for he found him attentive, studious, and intelligent — always the first to come to school, and the last to leave when school was over.

But he had one fault : he made too many friends ; and amongst them were several young rascals well known for their dislike to study and love of mischief.

The master warned him every day, and even the good Fairy never failed to tell him, and to repeat constantly : "Take care, Pinocchio ! Those bad schoolfellows of yours will end sooner or later by making you lose all love of study, and perhaps even they may bring upon you some great misfortune."

Now it happened that one fine day, as he was on his way to school, he met several of his usual companions who, coming up to him, asked : "Have you heard the great news ? "

"No."

"In the sea near here a Dog-fish has appeared as big as a mountain."

" Not really ? Can it be the same Dog-fish that was there when my poor papa was drowned ? "

" We are going to the shore to see him. Will you come with us ? "

" No ; I am going to school."

" What matters school ? We can go to school to-morrow. Whether we have a lesson more or a lesson less, we shall always remain the same donkeys."

" But what will the master say ? "

" The master may say what he likes. He is paid on purpose to grumble all day."

" And my mamma ? . . ."

" Mammas know nothing," answered those bad little boys.

" Do you know what I will do ? " said Pinocchio. " I have reasons for wishing to see the Dog-fish, but I will go and see him when school is over."

" Poor donkey ! " exclaimed one of the number. " Do you suppose that a fish of that size will wait your convenience ? As soon as he is tired of being here he will start for another place, and then it will be too late."

" How long does it take from here to the shore ? " asked the puppet.

" We can be there and back in an hour."

" Then away ! " shouted Pinocchio, " and he who runs fastest is the best ! "

Having thus given the signal to start, the boys, with their books and copy-books under their arms, rushed off across the fields, and Pinocchio was always the first—he seemed to have wings to his feet.

IX

WHEN he arrived on the shore Pinocchio looked out to sea ; but he saw no Dog-fish. The sea was as smooth as a great crystal mirror.

"Where is the Dog-fish ?" he asked, turning to his companions.

"He must have gone to have his breakfast," said one of them, laughing.

"Or he has thrown himself on to his bed to have a little nap," added another, laughing still louder.

From their absurd answers and silly laughter Pinocchio perceived that his companions had been making a fool of him. Taking it very badly he said to them angrily : "And now may I ask what fun you could find in deceiving me with the story of the Dog-fish ?"

"Oh, it was great fun !" answered the little rascals in chorus, "making you miss school, and persuading you to come with us. Are you not ashamed of being always so punctual and so diligent with your lessons ? Are you not ashamed of studying so hard ?"

"And if I study hard what concern is it of yours ?"

" It concerns us excessively, because it makes us appear in a bad light to the master. Boys who study make those who, like us, have no wish to learn seem worse by comparison. And that is too bad. We too have our pride ! . . ."

" Then what must I do to please you ? "

" You must follow our example and hate school, lessons, and the master—our three greatest enemies."

" And if I wish to continue my studies ? "

" In that case we will have nothing more to do with you, and at the first opportunity we will make you pay for it."

" Really," said the puppet, shaking his head, " you make me inclined to laugh."

" Eh, Pinocchio ! " shouted the biggest of the boys, confronting him. " None of your superior airs : don't come here to crow over us ! . . . for if you are not afraid of us, we are not afraid of you. Remember that you are one against seven of us."

" Seven, like the seven deadly sins," said Pinocchio with a shout of laughter.

" Listen to him ! He has insulted us all ! He called us the seven deadly sins ! . . ."

" Pinocchio ! beg our pardon . . . or it will be the worse for you ! . . ."

" Cuckoo ! " sang the puppet, putting his forefinger to the end of his nose scoffingly.

" Pinocchio ! it will end badly ! . . ."

" Cuckoo ! "

" You will get as many blows as a donkey ! . . ."

" Cuckoo ! "

" You will return home with a broken nose ! . . ."

" Cuckoo ! "

" Ah, you shall have the cuckoo from me ! " said the

most courageous of the boys. " Take that to begin with, and keep it for your supper to-night." And so saying he gave him a blow on the head with his fist.

But it was give and take ; for the puppet immediately returned the blow, and the fight in a moment became general and desperate.

Pinocchio, although he was one alone, defended himself like a hero. He used his feet, which were of the hardest wood, to such purpose that he kept his enemies at a respect-ful distance. Wherever they touched they left a bruise by way of reminder. The boys, becoming furious at not being able to measure themselves hand to hand with the puppet, had recourse to other weapons. Loosening their satchels they commenced throwing their school-books at him—grammars, dictionaries, spelling-books, geography books, and other scholastic works. But Pinocchio was quick and had sharp eyes, and always managed to duck in time, so that the books passed over his head and all fell into the sea.

Imagine the astonishment of the fish ! Thinking that the books were something to eat they all arrived in shoals, but having tasted a page or two, or a frontispiece, they spat it quickly out and made a wry face that seemed to say : " It isn't food for us ; we are accustomed to something much better ! "

Just then the boys, who had no more books of their own to throw, spied at a little distance the satchel that belonged to Pinocchio, and took possession of it. Amongst the books there was one bound in strong cardboard with the back and points of parchment. It was a Treatise on Arithmetic. One of the boys seized this volume, and aiming at Pinocchio's head threw it at him with all the force he could muster. But instead of hitting the puppet it struck one of his companions on the temple, who, turning as white as a sheet, said only : " Oh, mother, help . . . I am dying ! . . ." and fell his whole length on the sand. Thinking he was dead the terrified boys ran off as hard as their legs could carry them, and in a few minutes they were out of sight.

But Pinocchio remained. Although from grief and fright he was more dead than alive, nevertheless he ran and soaked his handkerchief in the sea and began to bathe the temples of his poor schoolfellow. Crying bitterly in his despair he kept calling him by name and saying to him : " Eugene ! . . . my poor Eugene ! . . . open your eyes and look at me ! . . . I did not do it, indeed it was not I that hurt you so ! believe me, it was not ! Open your eyes, Eugene. . . . Oh ! what shall I do ? how shall I ever return home ? How can I ever have the courage to go back to my good mamma ? What will become of me ? . . . Oh ! how much better it would have been, a thousand times better, if I had only gone to school ! . . . Why did I listen to my companions ? they have been my ruin. The master said to me, and my mamma repeated it often : ' Beware of bad companions ! ' But I am obstinate . . . a wilful fool. . . . I let them talk and then I always take my own way ! and I have to suffer for it. . . . And so, ever since I have been in the world, I have never had a happy quarter of an hour. Oh dear ! what will become of me, what will become of me, what will become of me ? . . ."

And Pinocchio began to cry and sob, and to strike his head with his fists, and to call poor Eugene by his name. Suddenly he heard the sound of approaching footsteps. He turned and saw two carabineers.

" What are you doing there lying on the ground ? " they asked Pinocchio.

" I am helping my schoolfellow."

" Has he been hurt ? "

" So it seems."

" Hurt indeed ! " said one of the carabineers, stooping down and examining Eugene closely. " This boy has been wounded in the temple. Who wounded him ? "

" Not I," stammered the puppet breathlessly.

" If it was not you, who then did it ? "

" Not I," repeated Pinocchio.

" And with what was he wounded ? "

" With this book." And the puppet picked up from the ground the Treatise on Arithmetic, bound in cardboard and parchment, and showed it to the carabineer.

" And to whom does this book belong ? "

" To me."

" That is enough : nothing more is wanted. Get up and come with us at once."

" But I am innocent. . . ."

" Come along with us ! "

Before they left, the carabineers called some fishermen, who were passing at that moment near the shore in their boat, and said to them :

" We give this boy who has been wounded in the head into your charge. Carry him to your house and nurse him. To-morrow we will come and see him."

They then turned to Pinocchio, and having placed him between them they said to him in a commanding voice : " Forward, and walk quickly ! "

The puppet set out along the road leading to the village. He was beside himself. He saw double : his legs shook : his tongue clung to the roof of his mouth, and he could not utter a word. And yet in the midst of his stupefaction and apathy his heart was pierced by a cruel thorn—the thought that he would have to pass under the windows of the good Fairy's house between the carabineers. He would rather have died.

They had already reached the village when a gust of wind blew Pinocchio's cap off his head and carried it ten yards off.

" Will you permit me," said the puppet to the carabineers, " to go and get my cap ? "

" Go then ; but be quick about it."

The puppet went and picked up his cap . . . but instead of putting it on his head he took it between his teeth and began to run as hard as he could towards the seashore.

The carabineers, thinking it would be difficult to overtake him, sent after him a large mastiff. Pinocchio ran, but the dog ran faster. He and the dog raised such clouds of dust that in a few minutes nothing could be seen of either of them.

You must know that Alidoro—for so the mastiff was called —ran so swiftly that he had nearly come up with Pinocchio. The puppet could hear the panting of the dreadful beast close behind him ; there was not a hand's breadth between them, he could even feel the dog's hot breath. Fortunately the shore was close and the sea but a few steps off. As soon as he reached the sands the puppet made a wonderful leap—a frog could have done no better—and plunged into the water.

Alidoro, on the contrary, wished to stop himself ; but carried away by the impetus of the race he also went into the sea. The unfortunate dog could not swim, and made great efforts to keep himself afloat with his paws ; but the more he struggled the farther he sank under the water.

When he rose to the surface again his eyes were rolling

with terror, and he barked out : " I am drowning ! I am drowning ! "

" Drown ! " shouted Pinocchio from a distance, seeing himself safe from all danger.

" Help me, dear Pinocchio ! . . . save me from death ! . . ."

At that agonising cry the puppet, who had in reality an excellent heart, was moved with compassion, and turning to the dog he said : " But if I save your life, will you promise not to run after me ? "

" I promise ! I promise ! Be quick, for pity's sake, for if you delay another half-minute I shall be dead."

Pinocchio hesitated : but remembering that his father had often told him that a good action is never lost, he swam to Alidoro, and taking hold of his tail with both hands brought him safe and sound on to the dry sand of the beach.

The poor dog could not stand. He had drunk, against his will, so much salt water that he was like a balloon. The puppet not wishing to trust him too far, thought it more prudent to jump again into the water. When he had swum some distance from the shore he called out to the friend he had rescued : " Good-bye, Alidoro ; a good journey to you, and take my compliments to all at home."

" Good-bye, Pinocchio," answered the dog ; " a thousand thanks for having saved my life. You have done me a great service, and in this world what is given is returned. If an occasion offers I shall not forget it."

Pinocchio swam on, keeping always near the land. At last he thought that he had reached a safe place. Giving a look along the shore he saw amongst the rocks a kind of cave from which a cloud of smoke was ascending.

" In that cave," he said to himself, " there must be a

fire. So much the better. I will go and dry and warm myself, and then ? . . . and then we shall see."

He approached the rocks ; but as he was going to climb up, he felt something under the water that rose higher and higher and carried him into the air. He tried to escape, but it was too late, for he found himself enclosed in a great net, together with a swarm of fish of every size and shape, who were flapping and struggling like so many despairing souls.

At the same moment a fisherman came out of the cave ; he was so ugly, so horribly ugly, that he looked like a sea monster. Instead of hair his head was covered with a thick bush of green grass, his skin was green, his eyes were green, his long beard that came down to the ground was also green. He had the appearance of an immense lizard standing on its hind-paws.

When the fisherman had drawn his net out of the sea, he exclaimed with great satisfaction : " Thank Heaven ! Again to-day I shall have a splendid feast of fish ! "

" What a mercy that I am not a fish ! " said Pinocchio to himself, regaining a little courage.

The net full of fish was carried into the cave, which was dark and smoky. In the middle of the cave a large frying-pan full of oil was frying, and sending out a smell of mushrooms that was suffocating.

" Now we will see what fish we have taken ! " said the green fisherman ; and putting into the net an enormous hand that looked like a baker's shovel, he pulled out a handful of mullet.

" These mullet are good ! " he said, looking at them and smelling them complacently. And after he had smelt them he threw them into a pan without water. He repeated the same operation many times ; and as he drew out the fish,

his mouth watered and he said, chuckling to himself :
" What good whiting ! . . . What exquisite sardines !
. . . These soles are delicious ! . . . And these crabs
excellent ! . . . What dear little anchovies ! . . ."

I need not tell you that the whiting, the sardines, the
soles, the crabs, and the anchovies were all thrown promis-
cuously into the pan to keep company with the mullet.
The last to remain in the net was Pinocchio.

No sooner had the fisherman taken him out than he
opened his big green eyes with astonishment, and cried,
half-frightened : " What species of fish is this ? Fish of
this kind I never remember to have eaten ! "

And he looked at him again attentively, and having
examined him well all over, he ended by saying : " I know :
he must be a craw-fish."

Pinocchio, mortified at being mistaken for a craw-fish,
said in an angry voice : " A craw-fish indeed ! what treat-
ment ! Let me tell you that I am a puppet."

" A puppet ? " replied the fisherman. " To tell the
truth, a puppet is quite a new fish for me. All the better !
I shall eat you with greater pleasure."

" Eat me ! but will you understand that I am not a fish ?
Do you hear that I talk and reason as you do ? "

" That is quite true," said the fisherman ; " and as I see
that you are a fish possessed of the talent of talking and
reasoning, I will treat you with all the attention that is your
due. In token of my friendship I will leave you the choice
of how you would like to be cooked."

" To tell the truth," answered Pinocchio. " if I am to
choose, I should prefer to be set at liberty and to return
home."

" You are joking ! Do you imagine that I would lose
the opportunity of tasting such a rare fish ? It is not every

day that a puppet fish is caught in these waters. I will fry you with the other fish, and you will be quite satisfied. It is always consolation to be fried in company."

At this speech the unhappy Pinocchio began to cry and scream and to implore for mercy; and he said, sobbing: "How much better it would have been if I had gone to school! . . . I would listen to my companions and now I am paying for it! Ih! . . . Ih! . . . Ih! . . ."

And he wriggled like an eel, and made efforts to slip out of the clutches of the green fisherman. But it was useless: the fisherman took a long strip of rush, and having bound his hands and feet as if he had been a sausage, he threw him into the pan with the other fish.

He then fetched a wooden bowl full of flour and began to flour them each in turn, and as soon as they were ready he threw them into the frying-pan.

The first to dance in the boiling oil were the poor whiting; the crabs followed, then the sardines, then the soles, then the anchovies, and at last it was Pinocchio's turn. Seeing himself so near death, and such a horrible death, he was so frightened, and trembled so violently, that he had neither voice nor breath left for further entreaties. But the poor boy implored with his eyes! The green fisherman, however, without caring in the least, plunged him five or six times in the flour, until he was white from head to foot, and looked like a puppet made of plaster.

Just as the fisherman was on the point of throwing Pinocchio into the frying-pan a large dog entered the cave, enticed there by the strong and savoury odour of fried fish.

"Get out!" shouted the fisherman threateningly, holding the floured puppet in his hand. But the poor dog, who was as hungry as a wolf, whined and wagged his tail as much as to say : " Give me a mouthful of fish and I will leave you in peace."

" Get out, I tell you ! " repeated the fisherman, and he stretched out his leg to give him a kick. But the dog, who, when he was really hungry, would not stand trifling, turned upon him, growling and showing his terrible tusks.

At that moment a little feeble voice was heard in the cave saying entreatingly : " Save me, Alidoro ! If you do not save me I shall be fried ! . . ."

The dog recognised Pinocchio's voice, and to his extreme surprise perceived that it proceeded from the floured bundle that the fisherman held in his hand. So he made a spring, seized the bundle in his mouth, and holding it gently between his teeth he rushed out of the cave and was gone like a flash of lightning. The fisherman, furious at seeing a fish he was so anxious to eat snatched from him, ran after the dog ; but he had not gone many steps when he was taken with a fit of coughing and had to give it up.

Alidoro, when he had reached the path that led to the village, stopped, and put his friend Pinocchio gently on the ground.

" How much I have to thank you for ! " said the puppet.

" There is no necessity," replied the dog. " You saved me and I have now returned it. You know that we must all help each other in this world. I was lying on the shore more dead than alive when the wind brought to me the smell of fried fish, and I followed it up. If I had arrived a second later . . ."

" Do not mention it ! " groaned Pinocchio, who was still trembling with fright.

Alidoro, laughing, extended his right paw to the puppet, who shook it heartily in token of great friendship, and they then separated.

The dog took the road home ; and Pinocchio, left alone, went to a cottage not far off, and said to a little old man who was warming himself in the sun : " Tell me, good man, do you know anything of a poor boy called Eugene who was wounded in the head ! . . ."

" The boy was brought by some fishermen to this cottage, and now . . ."

" And now he is dead ! . . ." interrupted Pinocchio with great sorrow.

" No, he is alive, and has returned to his home."

" Not really ? not really ? " cried the puppet, dancing with delight. " Then the wound was not serious ? . . ."

" It might have been very serious and even fatal," answered the little old man, " for they threw a thick book bound in cardboard at his head."

" And who threw it at him ? "

" One of his schoolfellows, a certain Pinocchio. . . ."

" And who is this Pinocchio ? " asked the puppet, pretending ignorance.

" They say that he is a bad boy, a vagabond, a regular good-for-nothing. . . ."

" Calumnies ! all calumnies ! "

" Do you know this Pinocchio ? "

" By sight ! " answered the puppet.

" And what is your opinion of him ? " asked the little man.

" He seems to me to be a very good boy, anxious to learn, and obedient and affectionate to his father and family. . . ."

Whilst the puppet was firing off all these lies, he touched his nose and perceived that it had lengthened more than a hand. Very much alarmed he began to cry out : " Don't believe, good man, what I have been telling you. I know Pinocchio very well, and I can assure you that he is really a very bad boy, disobedient and idle, who instead of going to school runs off with his companions to amuse himself."

He had hardly finished speaking when his nose became shorter and returned to the same size that it was before.

" And why are you all covered with white ? " asked the old man suddenly.

" I will tell you. . . . Without observing it I rubbed myself against a wall which had been freshly whitewashed," answered the puppet, ashamed to confess that he had been floured like a fish prepared for the frying-pan.

" And what have you done with your jacket, your trousers, and your cap ? "

" I met with robbers who took them from me. Tell me, good old man, could you perhaps give me some clothes to return home in ? "

" My boy, as to clothes, I have nothing but a little sack in which I keep beans. If you wish for it, take it ; there it is."

Pinocchio did not wait to be told twice. He took the sack at once, and with a pair of scissors he cut a hole at the end and at each side, and put it on like a shirt. And with this slight clothing he set off for the village. When he reached there it was night and very dark. A storm had come on, and as the rain was coming down in torrents he went straight to the Fairy's house, resolved to knock at the door, and hoping to be let in. But when he was there his courage failed him, and instead of knocking he ran away some twenty paces. He returned to the door a second time, but could not make up his mind ; he came back a third time, still he dared not ; the fourth time he laid hold of the knocker and, trembling, gave a little knock.

He waited and waited. At last, after half an hour had passed, a window on the top floor was opened—the house was four stories high—and Pinocchio saw a big Snail with a lighted candle on her head looking out. She called to him : " Who is there at this hour ? "

" Is the Fairy at home ? " asked the puppet.

" The Fairy is asleep and must not be awakened ; but who are you ? "

" Pinocchio."

" And who is Pinocchio ? "

" The puppet who lives in the Fairy's house."

" Ah, I understand ! " said the Snail. " Wait for me there. I will come down and open the door directly."

" Be quick, for pity's sake, for I am dying of cold."

" My boy, I am a snail, and snails are never in a hurry."

An hour passed, and then two, and the door was not opened. Pinocchio, who was wet through, and trembling from cold and fear, at last took courage and knocked again, and this time he knocked louder. At this second knock a window on the lower story opened, and the same Snail appeared at it.

" Beautiful little Snail," cried Pinocchio from the street, " I have been waiting for two hours ! And two hours on such a bad night seem longer than two years. Be quick, for pity's sake."

" My boy," answered the calm, phlegmatic little animal —" my boy, I am a snail, and snails are never in a hurry." And the window was shut again.

Shortly afterwards midnight struck ; then one o'clock, then two o'clock, and the door remained still closed. Pinocchio at last seized the knocker in a rage, intending to give a blow that would resound through the house. But the knocker, which was iron, turned suddenly into an eel, and slipping out of his hands disappeared in the stream of water that ran down the middle of the street.

" Ah ! is that it ? " shouted Pinocchio, blind with rage. And drawing a little back he gave a tremendous kick against the house door. The blow was indeed so violent that his foot went through the wood and stuck ; and when he tried to draw it back again it remained fixed.

Think of poor Pinocchio ! He was obliged to spend the remainder of the night with one foot on the ground and the other in the air. The following morning at daybreak the door was at last opened. That clever little Snail had taken only nine hours to come down from the fourth story to the house door. It was evident that her exertions must have been great.

" What are you doing with your foot stuck in the door ? " she asked the puppet, laughing.

" It was an accident. Do try, beautiful little Snail, if you cannot release me from this torture."

" My boy, that is the work of a carpenter, and I have never been a carpenter."

" Beg the Fairy from me ! . . ."

" The Fairy is asleep and must not be wakened."

" But what do you suppose that I can do all day nailed to this door ? "

" Amuse yourself by counting the ants that pass down the street."

" Bring me at least something to eat, for I am quite exhausted."

" At once," said the Snail.

In fact, after three hours and a half she returned to Pinocchio carrying a silver tray on her head. The tray contained a loaf of bread, a roast chicken, and four ripe apricots.

" Here is the breakfast that the Fairy has sent you," said the Snail.

The puppet felt very much comforted at the sight of these good things. But when he began to eat them, what was his disgust at making the discovery that the bread was plaster, the chicken cardboard, and the four apricots painted alabaster. He wanted to cry. In his desperation he tried to throw away the tray and all that was on it ; but instead, either from grief or exhaustion, he fainted away.

When he came to himself he found that he was lying on a sofa, and the Fairy was beside him.

" I will pardon you once more," the Fairy said, " but woe to you if you behave badly a third time ! . . ."

Pinocchio promised, and swore that he would study, and that for the future he would always conduct himself well. And he kept his word for the remainder of the year. Indeed, at the examinations before the holidays, he had the honour of being the first in the school, and his behaviour in general was so satisfactory and praiseworthy that the Fairy was very much pleased, and said to him : " To-morrow your wish shall be gratified : you shall cease to be a wooden puppet, and you shall become a boy."

No one who had not witnessed it could ever imagine Pinocchio's joy at this long-sighed-for good fortune. All his schoolfellows were to be invited for the following day to a grand breakfast at the Fairy's house, that they might celebrate together the great event. The Fairy had prepared two hundred cups of coffee and milk, and four hundred rolls cut and buttered on each side. The day promised to be most happy and delightful, but . . .

Unfortunately in the lives of puppets there is always a " but " that spoils everything.

X

PINOCCHIO, as was natural, asked the Fairy's permission to go round the town to make the invitations ; and the Fairy said to him : " Go if you like and invite your companions for the breakfast to-morrow, but remember to return home before dark. Have you understood ? "

" I promise to be back in an hour," answered the puppet.

" Take care, Pinocchio ! Boys are always very ready to promise ; but generally they are little given to keep their word."

" But I am not like other boys. When I say a thing, I do it."

" We shall see. If you are disobedient, so much the worse for you."

" Why ? "

" Because boys who do not listen to the advice of those who know more than they do always meet with some misfortune or other."

" I have experienced that," said Pinocchio. " But I shall never make that mistake again."

" We shall see if that is true."

Without saying more the puppet took leave of his good Fairy, who was like a mamma to him, and went out of the house singing and dancing. In less than an hour all his friends were invited. Some accepted at once heartily ; others at first required pressing ; but when they heard that the rolls to be eaten with the coffee were to be buttered on both sides, they ended by saying : " We will come also, to do you a pleasure."

Now I must tell you that amongst Pinocchio's friends and schoolfellows there was one that he greatly preferred and was very fond of. This boy's name was Romeo ; but he always went by the nickname of Candlewick, because he was so thin, straight, and bright like the new wick of a little night-light. Candlewick was the laziest and the naughtiest boy in the school ; but Pinocchio was devoted to him. He had indeed gone at once to his house to invite him to the breakfast, but he had not found him. He returned a second time, but Candlewick was not there. He went a third time, but it was in vain. Where could he search for him ? He looked here, there, and everywhere, and at last he saw him hiding in the porch of a peasant's cottage.

" What are you doing there ? " asked Pinocchio, coming up to him.

" I am waiting for midnight, to start . . ."

" Why, where are you going ? "

" Very far, very far, very far away."

" And I have been three times to your house to look for you."

" What did you want with me ? "

" Do you not know the great event ? Have you not heard of my good fortune ? "

" What is it ? "

" To-morrow I cease to be a puppet, and I become a boy like you, and like all the other boys."

" Much good may it do you."

"To-morrow, therefore, I expect you to breakfast at my house."

"But I tell you that I am going away to-night."

"And where are you going ?."

"I am going to live in a country . . . the most delightful country in the world; it is called the 'Land of Boobies.' Will you not come too ?"

"I ? No, never."

"Believe me, if you do not come you will repent it. Where could you find a better country for us boys ? There are no schools there : there are no masters : there are no books.   In that delightful land nobody ever studies. On Thursday there is never school; and every week consists of six Thursdays and one Sunday.   Only think, the autumn holidays begin on the 1st of January and finish on the last day of December.   That is the country for me ! . . ."

"But how are the days spent in the 'Land of Boobies' ?"

"They are spent in play and amusement from morning till night.   When night comes you go to bed, and recommence the same life in the morning.   What do you think of it ?"

"Hum ! . . ." said Pinocchio; and he shook his head slightly as much as to say, "That is a life that I also would willingly lead."

"Well, will you go with me ? Yes or no ? Resolve quickly."

"No, no, no, and again no.   I promised my good Fairy to become a well-conducted boy, and I will keep my word. And as I see that the sun is setting I must leave you at once and run away.   Good-bye, and a pleasant journey to you."

"Where are you rushing off to in such a hurry ?"

" Home. My good Fairy wishes me to be back before dark."

" Wait another two minutes."

" It will make me too late."

" Only two minutes."

" And if the Fairy scolds me ? "

" Let her scold. When she has scolded well she will hold her tongue," said that rascal Candlewick.

" And what are you going to do ? Are you going alone or with companions ? "

" Alone ? We shall be more than a hundred boys."

" And do you make the journey on foot ? "

" A coach will pass by shortly which is to take me to that happy country."

" What would I not give for the coach to pass by now that I might see you all start together."

" Stay here a little longer and you will see us."

" I have already delayed too long. The Fairy will be anxious about me."

" Poor Fairy ! Is she afraid that the bats will eat you ? "

" But now," continued Pinocchio, " are you really certain that there are no schools in that country ? . . ."

" Not even the shadow of one."

" And no masters either ? . . ."

" Not one."

" And no one is ever made to study ? "

" Never, never, never ! "

" What a delightful country ! " said Pinocchio, his mouth watering. " What a delightful country ! I have never been there, but I can quite imagine it. . . ."

" Why will you not come also ? "

" It is useless to tempt me. I promised my good Fairy to become a sensible boy, and I will not break my word.

Good-bye, Candlewick : a pleasant journey to you, amuse yourself, and think sometimes of your friends."

Thus saying the puppet made two steps to go, but then stopped, and turning to his friend he inquired : " But are you quite certain that in that country all the weeks consist of six Thursdays and one Sunday ? "

" Most certain."

" But do you know for certain that the holidays begin on the 1st of January and finish on the last day of December ? "

" Assuredly."

" What a delightful country ! " repeated Pinocchio, looking enchanted. Then, with a resolute air, he added in a great hurry : " This time really good-bye, and a pleasant journey to you."

" Good-bye."

" When do you start ? "

" Shortly."

" What a pity ! If really it wanted only an hour to the time of your start, I should be almost tempted to wait."

" And the Fairy ? "

" It is already late. . . . If I return home an hour sooner or an hour later it will be all the same."

" Poor Pinocchio ! And if the Fairy scolds you ? "

" I must have patience ! I will let her scold. When she has scolded well she will hold her tongue."

In the meantime night had come on and it was quite dark. Suddenly they saw in the distance a small light moving . . . and they heard a noise of talking, and the sound of a trumpet, but so small and feeble that it resembled the hum of a mosquito.

" Here it is ! " shouted Candlewick, jumping to his feet.

" What is it ? " asked Pinocchio in a whisper.

" It is the coach coming to take me. Now will you come, yes or no ? "

" But is it really true," asked the puppet, " that in that country boys are never obliged to study ? "

" Never, never, never ! "

" What a delightful country ! . . . What a delightful country ! . . . What a delightful country ! "

At last the coach arrived ; and it arrived without making the slightest noise, for its wheels were bound round with tow and rags. It was drawn by twelve pairs of donkeys. Some were gray, some white, some brindled like pepper and salt, and others had large stripes of yellow and blue.

But the most extraordinary thing was this : the twelve pairs, that is, the twenty-four donkeys, instead of being shod like other beasts of burden, had on their feet men's boots made of white kid.

The coachman was a little man broader than he was long, flabby and greasy like a lump of butter, with a small round face like an orange, a little mouth that was always laughing.

All the boys as soon as they saw him fell in love with him. The coach was in fact quite full of boys between eight and twelve years old, heaped one upon another like herrings in a barrel. They were uncomfortable, packed close together and could hardly breathe : but nobody said Oh !—nobody grumbled. The consolation of knowing that in a few hours they would reach a country where there were no books, no schools, and no masters, made them happy and resigned.

As soon as the coach had drawn up, the little man turned to Candlewick, and with a thousand smirks and grimaces said to him, smiling : " Tell me, my fine boy, would you also like to go to that fortunate country ? "

" I certainly wish to go."

" But I must warn you, my dear child, that there is not a place left in the coach. You can see for yourself that it is quite full. . . ."

" No matter," replied Candlewick ; " if there is no place inside, I will manage to sit on the springs."

And giving a leap he seated himself astride on the springs.

" And you, my love ! . . ." said the little man, turning in a flattering manner to Pinocchio, " what do you intend to do ? Are you coming with us, or are you going to remain behind ? "

" I remain behind," answered Pinocchio. " I am going home. I intend to study and to earn a good character at school, as all well-conducted boys do."

" Much good may it do you ! "

" Pinocchio ! " called out Candlewick, " listen to me : come with us and we shall have such fun."

" No, no, no ! "

" Come with us, and we shall have such fun," cried four other voices from the inside of the coach.

" Come with us, and we shall have such fun," shouted in chorus a hundred voices from the inside of the coach.

" But if I come with you, what will my good Fairy say ? " said the puppet, who was beginning to yield.

" Do not trouble your head with melancholy thoughts. Consider only that we are going to a country where we shall be at liberty to run riot from morning till night."

Pinocchio did not answer ; but he sighed : he sighed again : he sighed for the third time, and he said finally : " Make a little room for me, for I am coming too."

" The places are all full," replied the little man ; " but to show you how welcome you are, you shall have my seat on the box. . . ."

" And you ? . . ."

" Oh, I will go on foot."

" No, indeed, I could not allow that. I would rather mount one of these donkeys," cried Pinocchio.

Approaching the right-hand donkey of the first pair he attempted to mount him, but the animal suddenly kicked up his hind-legs, and backing violently threw the poor puppet into the middle of the road on to a heap of stones.

Roars of laughter followed; but the little man, instead of laughing, said to the puppet: " Mount him now without fear. That little donkey had got some whim into his head."

Pinocchio mounted, and the coach started. Whilst the donkeys were galloping and the coach was rattling over the stones of the high road, the puppet thought that he heard a low voice that was scarcely intelligible saying to him :

" Poor fool ! you would follow your own way, but you will repent it ! "

Pinocchio, feeling almost frightened, looked from side to side to try and discover where these words could come from : but he saw nobody. The donkeys galloped, the coach rattled, the boys inside slept, Candlewick snored like a dormouse, and the little man seated on the box sang between his teeth :

" During the night all sleep,
But I sleep never . . ."

After they had gone another mile, Pinocchio heard the same little low voice saying to him :

" Bear it in mind, simpleton ! Boys who refuse to study and turn their backs upon books, schools, and masters, to pass their time in play and amusement, sooner or later come to a bad end. . . . I know it by experience . . . and I can tell you. A day will come when you will weep as I am weeping now . . . but then it will be too late ! . . ."

On hearing these words whispered very softly the puppet, more frightened than ever, sprang down from the back of his donkey and went and took hold of his mouth.

Imagine his surprise when he found that the donkey was crying . . . and he was crying like a boy !

" Eh ! Sir coachman," cried Pinocchio to the little man, " here is an extraordinary thing ! This donkey is crying."

" Let him cry ; he will laugh when he is a bridegroom."

" But have you by chance taught him to talk ? "

" No ; but he spent three years in a company of learned dogs, and he learnt to mutter a few words."

" Poor beast ! "

" Come, come," said the little man, " don't let us waste time in seeing a donkey cry. Mount him, and let us go on : the night is cold and the road is long."

Pinocchio obeyed without another word. In the morning about daybreak they arrived safely in the " Land of Boobies."

It was a country unlike any other country in the world. The population was composed entirely of boys. The oldest were fourteen, and the youngest scarcely eight years old. In the streets there was such merriment, noise, and shouting, that it was enough to turn anybody's head. Some were playing with nuts, some with battledores, some with balls. Some rode bicycles, others wooden horses. A party were playing at hide and seek, a few were chasing each other. Some were amusing themselves with walking on their hands with their feet in the air. In every square, canvas theatres had been erected, and they were crowded with boys from morning till evening. On the walls of the houses there were inscriptions written in charcoal : " Long live playthings, we will have no more schools : down with arithmetic : " and similar other fine sentiments all in bad spelling.

Pinocchio, Candlewick, and the other boys who had made the journey with the little man, had scarcely set foot in the town before they were in the thick of the tumult, and I need not tell you that in a few minutes they had made acquaintance with everybody. Where could happier or more contented boys be found ?

In the midst of continual games and every variety of amusement, the hours, the days, and the weeks passed like lightning.

" Oh, what a delightful life ! " said Pinocchio, whenever by chance he met Candlewick.

" See, then, if I was not right ? " replied the other. " And to think that you did not want to come ! To think that you had taken it into your head to return home to your Fairy, and to lose your time in studying ! . . . If you are at this moment free from the bother of books and school, you must acknowledge that you owe it to me, to my advice and to my persuasions. It is only friends who know how to render such great services."

" It is true, Candlewick ! If I am now a really happy boy, it is all your doing. But do you know what the master used to say when he talked to me of you ? He always said to me : ' Do not associate with that rascal Candlewick, for he is a bad companion, and will only lead you into mischief ! . . .' "

" Poor master ! " replied the other, shaking his head. " I know only too well that he disliked me, and amused himself by calumniating me ; but I am generous and I forgive him ! "

"Noble soul!" said Pinocchio, embracing his friend affectionately, and kissing him between the eyes.

This delightful life had gone on for five months. The days had been entirely spent in play and amusement, without a thought of books or school, when one morning Pinocchio awoke to a most disagreeable surprise that put him into a very bad humour.

The surprise was that Pinocchio when he awoke scratched his head; and in scratching his head he discovered. . . . Can you guess in the least what he discovered?

He discovered to his great astonishment that his ears had grown more than a hand's length.

You know that the puppet from his birth had always had very small ears—so small that they were not visible to the naked eye. You can imagine then what he felt when he found that during the night his ears had become so long that they seemed like two brooms. He went at once in search of a glass that he might look at himself, but not being able to find one he filled the basin of his washing-stand with water, and he saw reflected what he certainly would never have wished to see. He saw his head embellished with a magnificent pair of donkey's ears!

Only think of poor Pinocchio's sorrow, shame, and despair!

He began to cry and roar, and he beat his head against the wall; but the more he cried the longer his ears grew: they grew, and grew, and became hairy towards the points.

At the sound of his loud outcries a beautiful little Marmot that lived on the first floor came into the room. Seeing the puppet in such grief she asked earnestly:

"What has happened to you, my dear fellow-lodger?"

"I am ill, my dear little Marmot, very ill . . . and of

an illness that frightens me. Do you understand counting a pulse ? "

" A little."

" Then feel and see if by chance I have got fever."

The little Marmot raised her right fore-paw ; and after having felt Pinocchio's pulse she said to him, sighing : " My friend, I am grieved to be obliged to give you bad news ! "

" What is it ? "

" You have got a very bad fever ! . . ."

" What fever is it ? "

" It is donkey fever."

" That is a fever that I do not understand," said the puppet, but he understood it only too well.

" Then I will explain it to you," said the Marmot. " You must know that in two or three hours you will be no longer a puppet, or a boy. . . ."

" Then what shall I be ? "

" In two or three hours you will become really and truly a little donkey, like those that draw carts and carry cabbages and salad to market."

" Oh ! unfortunate that I am ! unfortunate that I am ! " cried Pinocchio, seizing his two ears with his hands, and pulling them and tearing them furiously as if they had been some one else's ears.

" My dear boy," said the Marmot, by way of consoling him, " what can you do to prevent it ? It is destiny. It is written in the decrees of wisdom that all boys who are lazy, and who take a dislike to books, to schools, and to masters, and who pass their time in amusement, games, and diversions, must end sooner or later by becoming transformed into so many little donkeys."

" But it was not my fault : believe me, little Marmot, the fault was all Candlewick's ! . . ."

" And who is this Candlewick ? "

" One of my schoolfellows.   I wanted to return home :
I wanted to be obedient.   I wished to study and to earn
a good character . . . but Candlewick said to me : ' Why
should you bother yourself by studying ?   Why should
you go to school ? . . . Come with us instead to the
" Land of Boobies " : there we shall none of us have to
learn : there we shall amuse ourselves from morning to
night, and we shall always be merry.' "

" And why did you follow the advice of that false friend ?
of that bad companion ? "

" Why ? . . . Because, my dear little Marmot, I am a
puppet with no sense . . . and with no heart.   Ah ! if I
had had the least heart I should never have left that good
Fairy who loved me like a mamma, and who had done so
much for me ! . . . and I should be no longer a puppet
. . . for I should by this time have become a little boy
like so many others !   But if I meet Candlewick, woe to
him !   He shall hear what I think of him ! . . ."

And he turned to go out.   But when he reached the
door he remembered his donkey's ears, and feeling ashamed
to show them in public, what do you think he did ?   He
took a big cotton cap, and putting it on his head he pulled
it well down over the point of his nose.

He then set out, and went everywhere in search of
Candlewick.   He looked for him in the streets, in the
squares, in the little theatres, in every possible place ; but
he could not find him.   He inquired for him of everybody
he met, but no one had seen him.   He then went to seek
him at his house : and having reached the door he knocked.

" Who is there ? " asked Candlewick from within.

" It is I ! " answered the puppet.

" Wait a moment and I will let you in."

After half an hour the door was opened, and imagine Pinocchio's feelings when upon going into the room he saw his friend Candlewick with a big cotton cap on his head which came down over his nose.

At the sight of the cap Pinocchio felt almost consoled, and thought to himself :

" Has my friend got the same illness that I have ? Is he also suffering from donkey fever ? . . ."

And pretending to have observed nothing he asked him, smiling : " How are you, my dear Candlewick ? "

" Very well ; as well as a mouse in a Parmesan cheese."

" Excuse me ; but why, then, do you keep that cotton cap on your head which covers up your ears ? "

" The doctor ordered me to wear it because I have hurt this knee. And you, dear puppet, why have you got on that cotton cap pulled down over your nose ? "

" The doctor prescribed it because I have grazed my foot."

" Oh, poor Pinocchio ! . . ."

" Oh, poor Candlewick ! . . ."

After these words a long silence followed, during which the two friends did nothing but look mockingly at each other.

At last the puppet said in a soft mellifluous voice to his companion : " Satisfy my curiosity, my dear Candlewick : have you ever suffered from disease of the ears ? "

" Never ! . . . And you ? "

" Never ! Only since this morning one of my ears aches."

" Mine is also paining me."

" You also ? . . . And which of your ears hurts you ? "

" Both of them. And you ? "

" Both of them. Can we have got the same illness ? "

" I fear so."

" Will you let me see your ears ? "

" Why not ?   But first, my dear Pinocchio, I should like to see yours."

" No : you must be the first."

" No, dear !   First you and then I ! "

" Well," said the puppet, " let us come to an agreement like good friends.   We will both take off our caps at the same moment.   Do you agree ? "

" I agree."

" Then attention ! "

And Pinocchio began to count in a loud voice : " One ! Two ! Three ! "

At the word three ! the two boys took off their caps and threw them into the air.

And then a scene followed that would seem incredible if it was not true. That is, that when Pinocchio and Candlewick discovered that they were both struck with the same misfortune, instead of feeling full of mortification and grief, they began to prick their ungainly ears and to make a thousand antics, and they ended by going into bursts of laughter.   And they laughed, and laughed, until they had to hold themselves together. But in the midst of their merriment, Candlewick suddenly stopped, staggered, and changing colour said to his friend : " Help, help, Pinocchio ! "

" What is the matter with you ? "

" Alas, I cannot any longer stand upright."

" No more can I," exclaimed Pinocchio, tottering and beginning to cry.

And whilst they were talking they both doubled up and began to run round the room on their hands and feet. And as they ran, their hands became hoofs, their faces lengthened into muzzles, and their backs became covered with a light gray hairy coat sprinkled with black.

But do you know what was the worst moment for these two wretched boys? The worst and the most humiliating moment was when their tails grew. Vanquished by shame and sorrow they wept and lamented their fate.

Oh, if they had but been wiser! But instead of sighs and lamentations they could only bray like asses; and they brayed loudly and said in chorus: " ee-ah, ee-ah, ee-ah."

Whilst this was going on some one knocked at the door, and a voice on the outside said: " Open the door! I am the coachman, who brought you to this country. Open at once, or it will be the worse for you! "

Finding that the door remained shut the little man burst it open with a violent kick, and coming into the room he said to Pinocchio and Candlewick with his usual little laugh: " Well done, boys! You brayed well, and I recognised you by your voices. That is why I am here."

At these words the two little donkeys were quite stupefied, and stood with their heads down, their ears lowered, and their tails between their legs.

At first the little man stroked and caressed them; then taking out a currycomb he currycombed them well. And when by this process he had polished them till they shone like two mirrors, he put a halter round their necks and led them to the market-place, in hopes of selling them and making a good profit.

And indeed buyers were not wanting. Candlewick was bought by a peasant whose donkey had died the previous day. Pinocchio was sold to the director of a company of buffoons and tight-rope dancers, who bought him that he might teach him to leap and to dance with the other animals belonging to the company.

Pinocchio tried to learn how to jump through hoops, but each time that he came in front of the hoop, instead of going through it, he found it easier to go under it. At last he made a leap and went through it ; but his right leg unfortunately caught in the hoop, and that caused him to fall to the ground doubled up in a heap on the other side. When he got up he was lame, and it was only with great difficulty that he managed to return to the stable.

The following morning the veterinary, that is, the doctor of animals, paid him a visit, and declared that he was lame.

The director then said to the stable-boy : " What do you suppose I can do with a lame donkey ? He would eat food without earning it. Take him to the market and sell him."

When they reached the market a purchaser was found at once. He asked the stable-boy : " How much do you want for that lame donkey ? "

" Twenty francs."

" I will give you twenty pence. Don't suppose that I am buying him to make use of ; I am buying him solely for his skin. I see that his skin is very hard, and I intend to make a drum with it for the band of my village."

I leave it to my readers to imagine poor Pinocchio's feelings when he heard that he was destined to become a drum !

As soon as the purchaser had paid his twenty pence he conducted the little donkey to the seashore. He then put a stone round his neck, and tying a rope, the end of which he held in his hand, round his leg, he gave him a sudden push and threw him into the water.

Pinocchio, weighed down by the stone, went at once to the bottom ; and his owner, keeping tight hold of the cord, sat down quietly on a piece of rock to wait until the little donkey was drowned, intending then to skin him.

After Pinocchio had been fifty minutes under the water, his purchaser said aloud to himself : " My poor little lame donkey must by this time be quite drowned. I will therefore pull him out of the water, and I will make a fine drum of his skin."

And he began to haul in the rope that he had tied to the donkey's leg ; and he hauled, and hauled, and hauled, until at last . . . what do you think appeared above the water ? Instead of a little dead donkey he saw a live puppet, who was wriggling like an eel. Seeing this wooden puppet the poor man thought he was dreaming, and, struck dumb with astonishment, he remained with his mouth open and his eyes starting out of his head.

Having somewhat recovered from his first stupefaction, he asked in a quavering voice : " And the little donkey that I threw into the sea ? What has become of him ? "

" I am the little donkey ! " said Pinocchio, laughing.

" You ? "

" I."

" Ah, you young scamp ! Do you dare to make game of me ? "

" To make game of you ? Quite the contrary, my dear master ; I am speaking seriously."

" But how can you, who, but a short time ago, were a little donkey, have become a wooden puppet, only from having been left in the water ? "

" It must have been the effect of sea-water. The sea makes extraordinary changes."

" Beware, puppet, beware ! . . . Don't imagine that you can amuse yourself at my expense. Woe to you, if I lose patience ! . . ."

" Well, master, do you wish to know the true story ? If you will set my leg free I will tell it you."

The good man, who was curious to hear the true story, immediately untied the knot that kept him bound ; and Pinocchio, finding himself as free as a bird in the air, commenced as follows :

" You must know that I was once a puppet as I am now, and I was on the point of becoming a boy like the many that there are in the world. But instead, induced by my dislike to study, and the advice of bad companions, I ran away from home . . . and one fine day when I awoke I found myself changed into a donkey with long ears . . . and a long tail ! . . . What a disgrace it was to me ! Taken to the market to be sold I was bought by the director of an equestrian company, who took it into his head to make a famous dancer of me. But I had a bad fall and lamed both my legs.   Then the director, not knowing what to do with a lame donkey, sent me to be sold, and you were the purchaser ! . . ."

" Only too true ! And I paid twenty pence for you. And now who will give me back my poor pennies ? "

" And why did you buy me ? You bought me to make a drum of my skin ! . . . a drum ! . . ."

" Only too true ! And now where shall I find another skin ? . . ."

" Don't despair, master. There are such a number of little donkeys in the world ! "

" Tell me, you impertinent rascal, does your story end here ? "

" No," answered the puppet ; " I have another two words to say and then I shall have finished. After you had bought me you brought me to this place to kill me ; but then, yielding to a feeling of compassion, you preferred to tie a stone round my neck and to throw me into the sea. This humane feeling does you great honour, and I shall always be grateful to you for it. But nevertheless, dear master, this time you made your calculations without considering the Fairy ! . . ."

" And who is this Fairy ? "

" She is my mamma, and she resembles all other good mammas who care for their children, and who never lose sight of them, but help them lovingly, even when, on account of their foolishness and evil conduct, they deserve to be abandoned and left to themselves. Well, then, the good Fairy, as soon as she saw that I was in danger of drowning, sent immediately an immense shoal of fish, who, believing me really to be a little dead donkey, began to eat me. And what mouthfuls they took ! I should never have thought that fish were greedier than boys ! . . . Some ate my ears, some my muzzle, others my neck and mane, some the skin of my legs, some my coat . . . and amongst them there was a little fish so polite that he even condescended to eat my tail."

" From this time forth," said his purchaser, horrified, " I swear that I will never touch fish. It would be too dreadful to open a mullet, or a fried whiting, and to find inside a donkey's tail ! "

" I agree with you," said the puppet, laughing. " However, I must tell you that when the fish had finished eating the donkey's hide that covered me from head to foot, they naturally reached the bone . . . or rather the wood, for as you see I am made of the hardest wood. But after giving a few bites they soon discovered that I was not a morsel for their teeth, and, disgusted with such indigestible food, they went off, some in one direction and some in another, without so much as saying thank you to me.

And now, at last, I have told you how it was that when you pulled up the rope you found a live puppet instead of a dead donkey."

" I laugh at your story," cried the man in a rage. " I know only that I spent twenty pence to buy you, and I will have my money back. Shall I tell you what I will do ? I will take you back to the market and sell you as seasoned wood for lighting fires."

" Sell me if you like ; I am content," said Pinocchio.

But as he said it he made a spring and plunged into the water. Swimming gaily away he called to his poor owner : " Good-bye, master ; if you should be in want of a skin to make a drum, remember me."

And he laughed and went on swimming ; and after a while he turned again and shouted louder : " Good-bye, master ; if you should be in want of a little well-seasoned wood for lighting the fire, remember me."

In the twinkling of an eye he had swum so far off that he was scarcely visible. All that could be seen of him was a little black speck on the surface of the sea that from time to time lifted its legs out of the water and leapt and capered like a dolphin enjoying himself.

Whilst Pinocchio was swimming he knew not whither he saw in the midst of the sea a rock that seemed to be made of white marble, and on the summit there stood a beautiful little goat who bleated lovingly and made signs to him to approach. But the most singular thing was this. The little goat's hair, instead of being white or black, or a mixture of two colours as is usual with other goats, was blue, and of a very vivid blue, greatly resembling the hair of the beautiful Child.

I leave you to imagine how rapidly poor Pinocchio's heart began to beat. He swam with redoubled strength and energy towards the white rock; and he was already half-way when he saw, rising up out of the water and coming to meet him, the horrible head of a sea-monster. His wide-open cavernous mouth and his three rows of enormous teeth would have been terrifying to look at even in a picture.

This sea-monster was neither more nor less than that gigantic Dog-fish who has been mentioned many times in this story.

Only think of poor Pinocchio's terror at the sight of the monster. He tried to avoid it, to change his direction; he tried to escape; but that immense wide-open mouth came towards him with the velocity of an arrow.

"Be quick, Pinocchio, for pity's sake," cried the beautiful little goat, bleating.

And Pinocchio swam desperately with his arms, his chest, his legs, and his feet.

"Quick, Pinocchio, the monster is close upon you! . . ."

And Pinocchio swam quicker than ever, and flew on with the rapidity of a ball from a gun. He had nearly reached the rock, and the little goat, leaning over towards the sea, had stretched out her fore-legs to help him out of the water! . . .

But it was too late! The monster had overtaken him, and, drawing in his breath, he sucked in the poor puppet as he would have sucked a hen's egg; and he swallowed him with such violence and avidity that Pinocchio, in falling into the Dog-fish's stomach, received such a blow that he remained unconscious for a quarter of an hour afterwards.

When he came to himself again after the shock he could not in the least imagine in what world he was. All round him it was quite dark, and the darkness was so black and so profound that it seemed to him that he had fallen head downwards into an inkstand full of ink. He listened, but he could hear no noise ; only from time to time great gusts of wind blew in his face. At first he could not understand where the wind came from, but at last he discovered that it came out of the monster's lungs. For you must know that the Dog-fish suffered very much from asthma, and when he breathed it was exactly as if a north wind was blowing.

Pinocchio at first tried to keep up his courage ; but when he had one proof after another that he was really shut up in the body of this sea-monster he began to cry and scream and to sob out : " Help ! help ! Will nobody come to save me ? "

" Who do you think could save you, unhappy wretch ? . . ." said a voice in the dark that sounded like a guitar out of tune.

" Who is speaking ? " asked Pinocchio, frozen with terror.

" It is I ! I am a poor Tunny who was swallowed by the Dog-fish at the same time that you were. And what fish are you ? "

" I have nothing in common with fish. I am a puppet."

" Then if you are not a fish, why did you let yourself be swallowed by the monster ? "

" I didn't let myself be swallowed : it was the monster swallowed me ! And now, what are we to do here in the dark ? "

" Resign ourselves and wait until the Dog-fish has digested us both."

" But I do not want to be digested ! " howled Pinocchio, beginning to cry again.

" Neither do I want to be digested," added the Tunny ; " but I am enough of a philosopher to console myself by thinking that when one is born a Tunny it is more dignified to die in the water than in oil."

" That is all nonsense ! " cried Pinocchio.

" It is my opinion," replied the Tunny ; " and opinions, so say the political Tunnies, ought to be respected."

" To sum it all up . . . I want to get away from here . . . I want to escape."

" Escape if you are able ! . . ."

" Is this Dog-fish who has swallowed us very big ? " asked the puppet.

" Big ! Why, only imagine, his body is two miles long without counting his tail."

Whilst they were holding this conversation in the dark, Pinocchio thought that he saw a light a long way off.

" What is that little light I see in the distance ? " he asked.

" It is most likely some companion in misfortune who is waiting like us to be digested."

" I will go and find him. Do you not think that it may by chance be some old fish who perhaps could show us how to escape ? "

" I hope it may be so with all my heart, dear puppet."

" Good-bye, Tunny."

" Good-bye, puppet, and good fortune attend you."

" Where shall we meet again ? . . ."

" Who can say ? . . . It is better not even to think of it ! "

XI

PINOCCHIO, having taken leave of his friend the Tunny, began to grope his way in the dark through the body of the Dog-fish, taking a step at a time in the direction of the light that he saw shining dimly at a great distance.

The farther he advanced the brighter became the light; and he walked and walked until at last he reached it : and when he reached it . . . what did he find ? He found a little table spread out, and on it a lighted candle stuck into a green glass bottle, and seated at the table was a little old man. He was eating some live fish, and they were so very much alive that whilst he was eating them they sometimes even jumped out of his mouth.

At this sight Pinocchio was filled with such great and unexpected joy that he became almost delirious. He wanted to laugh, he wanted to cry, he wanted to say a thousand things, and instead he could only stammer out a few confused and broken words. At last he succeeded in uttering a cry of joy, and opening his arms he threw them round the little old man's neck, and began to shout : " Oh, my dear papa ! I have found you at last ! I will never leave you more, never more, never more ! "

" Then my eyes tell me true ? " said the little old man, rubbing his eyes; "then you are really my dear Pinocchio?"

" Yes, yes, I am Pinocchio, really Pinocchio ! And

you have quite forgiven me, have you not ? Oh, my dear papa, how good you are ! . . . and to think that I, on the contrary . . . Oh ! but if you only knew what misfortunes have been poured on my head, and all that has befallen me ! Only imagine, the day that you, poor dear papa, sold your coat to buy me a Spelling-book that I might go to school, I escaped to see the puppet-show, and the showman wanted to put me on the fire, that I might roast his mutton, and he was the same that afterwards gave me five gold pieces to take them to you, but I met the Fox and the Cat, who took me to the inn of the Red Craw-fish, where they ate like wolves, and I left by myself in the middle of the night, and I encountered assassins who ran after me, and I ran away, and they followed, and I ran, and they always followed me, and I ran, until they hung me to a branch of a Big Oak, and the beautiful Child with blue hair sent a little carriage to fetch me, and the doctors when they had seen me said immediately, ' If he is not dead, it is a proof that he is still alive '—and then by chance I told a lie, and my nose began to grow until I could no longer get through the door of the room, for which reason I went with the Fox and the Cat to bury the four gold pieces, for one I had spent at the inn, and instead of two thousand gold pieces I found none left, for which reason the judge when he heard that I had been robbed had me immediately put in prison to content the robbers, and then when I was coming away I saw a beautiful bunch of grapes in a field, and I was caught in a trap, and the peasant, who was quite right, put a dog-collar round my neck that I might guard the poultry-yard, and acknowledging my innocence let me go, and so I returned to the house of the beautiful Child who was dead, and the Pigeon, seeing that I was crying, said to me, ' I have seen your father who was building a little boat to go in search of you,' and I said to him, ' Oh ! if I had also wings,' and he said to me, ' Do you want to go to your father ? ' and I said, ' Without doubt ! but who will take me to him ? ' and he said to me, ' I will take you,' and I said to him, ' How ? ' and he said to me, ' Get on my back,' and so we flew all night, and then in the morning all the fishermen who were looking out to sea said to me, ' There is a poor man in a boat who is on the point of being drowned,' and I recognised you at once, even at that distance, for my heart told me, and I made signs to you to return to land. . . .''

" I also recognised you," said Geppetto, " and I would willingly have returned to the shore : but what was I to do ! The sea was tremendous, and a great wave upset my boat. Then a horrible Dog-fish who was near, as soon as he saw me in the water, came towards me, and putting out his tongue took hold of me, and swallowed me as if I had been a little Bologna tart."

" And how long have you been shut up here ? " asked Pinocchio.

" Since that day—it must be nearly two years ago : two years, my dear Pinocchio, that have seemed to me like two centuries ! "

" And how have you managed to live ? And where did you get the candle ? And the matches to light it ? Who gave them to you ? "

" Stop, and I will tell you everything. You must know, then, that in the same storm in which my boat was upset a merchant vessel foundered. The sailors were all saved, but the vessel went to the bottom, and the Dog-fish, who had that day an excellent appetite, after he had swallowed me, swallowed also the vessel. . . ."

" How ? "

" He swallowed it in one mouthful, and the only thing that he spat out was the mainmast, that had stuck between his teeth like a fish-bone. Fortunately for me the vessel was laden with preserved meat in tins, biscuit, bottles of wine, dried raisins, cheese, coffee, sugar, candles, and boxes of wax matches. With this providential supply I have been able to live for two years. But I have arrived at the end of my resources : there is nothing left in the larder, and this candle that you see burning is the last that remains. . . ."

" And after that ¿ "

" After that, dear boy, we shall both remain in the dark."

" Then, dear little papa," said Pinocchio, " there is no time to lose. We must think of escaping. . . ."

" Of escaping ¿ . . . and how ¿ "

" We must escape through the mouth of the Dog-fish, throw ourselves into the sea and swim away."

" You talk well : but, dear Pinocchio, I don't know how to swim."

" What does that matter ¿ . . . I am a good swimmer, and you can get on my shoulders and I will carry you safely to shore."

" All illusions, my boy ! " replied Geppetto, shaking his head, with a melancholy smile. " Do you suppose it possible that a puppet like you, scarcely a metre high, could have the strength to swim with me on his shoulders ! "

" Try it and you will see ! "

Without another word Pinocchio took the candle in his hand, and going in front to light the way, he said to his father : " Follow me, and don't be afraid."

And they walked for some time and traversed the body and the stomach of the Dog-fish. But when they had arrived at the point where the monster's big throat began they thought it better to stop to give a good look round and to choose the best moment for escaping.

Now I must tell you that the Dog-fish, being very old, and suffering from asthma and palpitation of the heart, was obliged to sleep with his mouth open. Pinocchio, therefore, having approached the entrance to his throat, looking up could see beyond the enormous gaping mouth a large piece of starry sky and beautiful moonlight.

" This is the moment to escape," he whispered, turning to his father ; " the Dog-fish is sleeping like a dormouse, the sea is calm, and it is as light as day. Follow me, dear papa, and in a short time we shall be in safety."

They immediately climbed up the throat of the sea-monster, and having reached his immense mouth they began to walk on tiptoe down his tongue.

Before taking the final leap the puppet said to his father : " Get on my shoulders and put your arms tight round my neck. I will take care of the rest."

As soon as Geppetto was firmly settled on his son's shoulders, Pinocchio, feeling sure of himself, threw himself into the water and began to swim. The sea was as smooth as oil, the moon shone brilliantly, and the Dog-fish was sleeping so profoundly that even a cannonade would have failed to wake him.

Whilst Pinocchio was swimming quickly towards the shore he discovered that his father, who was on his shoulders with his legs in the water, was trembling as violently as if the poor man had got an attack of ague fever.

Was he trembling from cold or from fear ? . . . Perhaps a little from both the one and the other. But Pinocchio, thinking that it was from fear, said to comfort him : " Courage, papa ! In a few minutes we shall be safely on shore."

" But where is this blessed shore ? " asked the little old man, becoming still more frightened, and screwing up his eyes as tailors do when they wish to thread a needle. " I have been looking in every direction and I see nothing but the sky and the sea."

" But I see the shore as well," said the puppet. " You must know that I am like a cat : I see better by night than by day."

Poor Pinocchio was making a pretence of being in good spirits, but in reality . . . in reality he was beginning to feel discouraged : his strength was failing, he was gasping and panting for breath . . . he could do no more, and the shore was still far off.

He swam until he had no breath left ; then he turned his head to Geppetto and said in broken words :

" Papa . . . help me . . . I am dying ! . . ."

The father and son were on the point of drowning when they heard a voice like a guitar out of tune saying : " Who is it that is dying ? "

" It is I, and my poor father ! . . ."

" I know that voice ! You are Pinocchio ! "

" Precisely : and you ? "

" I am the Tunny, your prison companion in the body of the Dog-fish."

" And how did you manage to escape ? "

" I followed your example. You showed me the road, and I escaped after you."

" Tunny, you have arrived at the right moment ! I implore you to help us, or we are lost."

" Willingly. You must take hold of my tail and leave me to guide you. I will take you on shore in four minutes."

Geppetto and Pinocchio accepted the offer at once ; but instead of holding on by his tail they thought it would be more comfortable to get on the Tunny's back.

Having reached the shore Pinocchio sprang first on land that he might help his father to do the same. He then turned to the Tunny, and said to him in a voice full of emotion : " My friend, you have saved my papa's life. I can find no words with which to thank you properly. Permit me at least to give you a kiss as a sign of my eternal gratitude ! . . ."

The Tunny put his head out of the water, and Pinocchio, kneeling on the ground, kissed him tenderly on the mouth. At this spontaneous proof of warm affection, the poor Tunny, who was not accustomed to it, felt extremely touched, and ashamed to let himself be seen crying like a child, he plunged under the water and disappeared.

By this time the day had dawned. Pinocchio then offering his arm to Geppetto, who had scarcely breath to stand, said to him : " Lean on my arm, dear papa, and let us go. We will walk very slowly like the ants, and when we are tired we can rest by the wayside."

" And where shall we go ? " asked Geppetto.

" In search of some house or cottage, where they will give us for charity a mouthful of bread, and a little straw to serve as a bed."

They had not gone a hundred yards when they saw by the roadside two villainous-looking individuals begging.

They were the Cat and the Fox, but they were scarcely recognisable. Fancy ! the Cat had so long feigned blindness that she had become blind in reality ; and the Fox, old, mangy, and with one side paralysed, had not even his tail left. That sneaking thief, having fallen into the most squalid misery, one fine day had found himself obliged to sell his beautiful tail to a travelling pedlar, who bought it to drive away flies.

" Oh, Pinocchio ! " cried the Fox, " give a little in charity to two poor infirm people."

" Infirm people," repeated the Cat.

" Begone, impostors ! " answered the puppet. " You took me in once, but you will never catch me again."

" Believe me, Pinocchio, we are now poor and unfortunate indeed ! "

" If you are poor, you deserve it. Recollect the proverb: ' Stolen money never fructifies.' Begone, impostors."

And thus saying Pinocchio and Geppetto went their way. When they had gone another hundred yards they saw, at the end of a path in the middle of the fields, a nice little straw hut with a roof of tiles and bricks.

" That hut must be inhabited by some one," said Pinocchio. " Let us go and knock at the door."

They went and knocked.

" Who is there ? " said a little voice from within.

" We are a poor father and son without bread and without a roof," answered the puppet.

" Turn the key and the door will open," said the same little voice.

Pinocchio turned the key and the door opened. They went in and looked here, there, and everywhere, but could see no one.

" Oh ! where is the master of the house ? " said Pinocchio, much surprised.

" Here I am up here ! "

The father and son looked immediately up to the ceiling, and there on a beam they saw the Talking-cricket.

" Oh, my dear little Cricket ! " said Pinocchio, bowing politely to him.

" Ah ! now you call me ' Your dear little Cricket.' But

do you remember the time when you threw the handle of a hammer at me, to drive me from your house ? . . ."

" You are right, Cricket ! Drive me away also . . . throw the handle of a hammer at me ; but have pity on my poor papa. . . ."

" I will have pity on both father and son, but I wished to remind you of the ill-treatment I received from you, to teach you that in this world, when it is possible, we should show courtesy to everybody, if we wish it to be extended to us in our hour of need."

" You are right, Cricket, you are right, and I will bear in mind the lesson you have given me. But tell me how you managed to buy this beautiful hut."

" This hut was given to me yesterday by a goat whose wool was of a beautiful blue colour."

" And where has the goat gone ? " asked Pinocchio with lively curiosity.

" I do not know."

" And when will it come back ? . . ."

" It will never come back. It went away yesterday in great grief, and, bleating, it seemed to say : ' Poor Pinocchio . . . I shall never see him more . . . by this time the Dog-fish must have devoured him ! . . .' "

" Did it really say that ? . . . Then it was she ! . . . it was my dear little Fairy . . ." exclaimed Pinocchio, crying and sobbing.

When he had cried for some time he dried his eyes, and prepared a comfortable bed of straw for Geppetto to lie down upon. Then he asked the Cricket : " Tell me, little Cricket, where can I find a tumbler of milk for my poor papa ? "

" Three fields off from here there lives a gardener called Giangio who keeps cows. Go to him and you will get the milk you are in want of."

Pinocchio ran all the way to Giangio's house ; and the gardener asked him : " How much milk do you want ? "

" I want a tumblerful."

" A tumbler of milk costs a halfpenny. Begin by giving me the halfpenny."

" I have not even a farthing," replied Pinocchio, grieved and mortified.

" That is bad, puppet," answered the gardener. " If you have not even a farthing, I have not even a drop of milk."

" I must have patience ! " said Pinocchio, and he turned to go.

" Wait a little," said Giangio. " We can come to an arrangement together. Will you undertake to turn the pumping machine ? "

" What is the pumping machine ? "

" It is a wooden pole which serves to draw up the water from the cistern to water the vegetables."

" You can try me. . . ."

" Well, then, if you will draw a hundred buckets of water, I will give you in compensation a tumbler of milk."

" It is a bargain."

Giangio then led Pinocchio to the kitchen garden and taught him how to turn the pumping machine. Pinocchio immediately began to work ; but before he had drawn up the hundred buckets of water the perspiration was pouring from his head to his feet. Never before had he undergone such fatigue.

"Up till now," said the gardener, " the labour of turning the pumping machine was performed by my little donkey ; but the poor animal is dying."

" Will you take me to see him ? " said Pinocchio.

" Willingly."

When Pinocchio went into the stable he saw a beautiful little donkey stretched on the straw, worn out from hunger and overwork.   After looking at him earnestly he said to himself, much troubled : " I am sure I know this little donkey !   His face is not new to me."

And bending over him he asked him in asinine language : " Who are you ? "

At this question the little donkey opened his dying eyes, and answered in broken words in the same language :

" I am . . . Can . . . dle . . . wick. . . ."

And having again closed his eyes he expired.

" Oh, poor Candlewick ! " said Pinocchio in a low voice ; and taking a handful of straw he dried a tear that was rolling down his face.

" Do you grieve for a donkey that cost you nothing ? " said the gardener.   " What must it be to me who bought him for ready money ? "

" I must tell you . . . he was my friend ! "

" Your friend ? "

" One of my schoolfellows ! . . ."

" How ? " shouted Giangio, laughing loudly.   " How ? had you donkeys for schoolfellows ? . . . I can imagine what wonderful studies you must have made ! . . ."

The puppet, who felt much mortified at these words, did not answer ; but taking his tumbler of milk, still quite warm, he returned to the hut.

And from that day for more than five months he continued to get up at daybreak every morning to go and turn the pumping machine, to earn the tumbler of milk that was of such benefit to his father in his bad state of health. Nor was he satisfied with this ; for during the time that he had over he learnt to make hampers and baskets of rushes, and with the money he obtained by selling them he was able with great economy to provide for all the daily expenses. Amongst other things he constructed an elegant little wheel-chair, in which he could take his father out on fine days to breathe a mouthful of fresh air.

By his industry, ingenuity, and his anxiety to work and to overcome difficulties, he not only succeeded in maintaining his father, who continued infirm, in comfort, but he also contrived to put aside forty pence to buy himself a new coat.

One morning he said to his father : " I am going to the neighbouring market to buy myself a jacket, a cap, and a pair of shoes. When I return," he added, laughing, " I shall be so well dressed that you will take me for a fine gentleman."

And leaving the house he began to run merrily and happily along. All at once he heard himself called by name, and turning round he saw a big Snail crawling out from the hedge.

" Do you not know me ? " asked the Snail.

" It seems to me . . . and yet I am not sure . . ."

" Do you not remember the Snail who was lady's-maid to the Fairy with blue hair ? Do you not remember the time when I came downstairs to let you in, and you were caught by your foot which you had stuck through the house door ? "

" I remember it all," shouted Pinocchio. " Tell me quickly, my beautiful little Snail, where have you left my good Fairy ? What is she doing ? has she forgiven me ? does she still remember me ? does she still wish me well ? is she far from here ? can I go and see her ? "

To all these rapid, breathless questions the Snail replied in her usual phlegmatic manner : " My dear Pinocchio, the poor Fairy is lying in bed at the hospital ! . . ."

" At the hospital ? . . ."

" It is only too true. Overtaken by a thousand mis-fortunes she has fallen seriously ill, and she has not even enough to buy herself a mouthful of bread."

" Is it really so ? . . . Oh, what sorrow you have given me ! Oh, poor Fairy ! poor Fairy ! poor Fairy ! . . . If I had a million I would run and carry it to her . . . but I have only forty pence . . . here they are : I was going to buy a new coat. Take them, Snail, and carry them at once to my good Fairy."

" And your new coat ? . . ."

" What matters my new coat ? I would sell even these rags that I have got on to be able to help her. Go, Snail, and be quick ; and in two days return to this place, for I hope I shall then be able to give you some more money. Up to this time I have worked to maintain my papa : from to-day I will work five hours more that I may also maintain my good mamma. Good-bye, Snail, I shall expect you in two days."

The Snail, contrary to her usual habits, began to run like a lizard in a hot August sun.

That evening Pinocchio, instead of going to bed at ten o'clock, sat up till midnight had struck ; and instead of making eight baskets of rushes he made sixteen.

Then he went to bed and fell asleep. And whilst he slept he thought that he saw the Fairy smiling and beautiful, who, after having kissed him, said to him : " Well done, Pinocchio ! To reward you for your good heart I will forgive you for all that is past. Boys who minister tenderly to their parents are deserving of great praise and affection. Try and do better in the future and you will be happy."

At this moment his dream ended, and Pinocchio opened his eyes and awoke.

But imagine his astonishment when upon awakening

he discovered that he was no longer a wooden puppet, but that he had become instead a boy, like all other boys. He gave a glance round and saw that the straw walls of the hut had disappeared, and that he was in a pretty little room furnished and arranged with a simplicity that was almost elegance. Jumping out of bed he found a new suit of clothes ready for him, a new cap, and a pair of new leather boots that fitted him beautifully.

He was hardly dressed when he naturally put his hands in his pockets, and pulled out a little ivory purse on which these words were written : " The Fairy with the blue hair returns the forty pence to her dear Pinocchio, and thanks him for his good heart." He opened the purse, and instead of forty copper pennies, he saw forty shining gold pieces fresh from the mint.

He then went and looked at himself in the glass, and he thought he was some one else. For he no longer saw the usual reflection of a wooden puppet ; he was greeted instead by the image of a bright intelligent boy with chestnut hair, blue eyes, and looking as happy and joyful as if it were the Easter holidays.

In the midst of all these wonders succeeding each other Pinocchio felt quite bewildered, and he could not tell if he was really awake or if he was dreaming with his eyes open.

" Where can my papa be ? " he exclaimed suddenly, and going into the next room he found old Geppetto quite well, lively, and in good humour, just as he had been formerly. He had already resumed his trade of wood-carving, and he was designing a rich and beautiful frame of leaves, flowers, and the heads of animals.

" Satisfy my curiosity, dear papa," said Pinocchio, throwing his arms round his neck and covering him with kisses ; " how can this sudden change be accounted for ? "

" This sudden change in our home is all your doing," answered Geppetto.

" How my doing ? "

" Because when boys who have behaved badly turn over a new leaf and become good, they have the power of bringing content and happiness to their families."

Pinocchio said to himself with great complacency : " How ridiculous I was when I was a puppet ! and how glad I am that I have become a well-behaved little boy ! . . ."